THE STORYTELLER

Kate Armstrong

Holland House

Paperback ISBN: 978-1-910688-06-9
Kindle: 978-1-910688-07-6

Cover picture: Seated Girl by Ernst Ludwig Kirchner
Cover design by Ken Dawson, Creative Covers

Typeset by handebooks.co.uk

Published in the USA and UK

Holland House Books
Holland House
47 Greenham Road
Newbury, Berkshire RG14 7HY
United Kingdom

www.hhousebooks.com

FOR MATTHEW

SUMMER

I

Shall we start again?

Sit back in your chair; relax; tuck that greasy strand of hair behind your ear (yes, tie your crude ponytail again if you wish—we have time, my dear, we have time); breathe in, breathe out, and wait. We are ready? We are ready. Now, tell me what you want to say.

Silence. You look away. Stillness. For a moment also lost, I also pause.

Then, let me help, I say, taking clear adult charge. It would be usual, I say, to start at the beginning: full name, date of birth, parents' names. But we could, if you prefer, take the oblique approach. You could give me an anecdote, an episode, a moment of truth. How about your first kiss? Not told crudely, of course, but detail would be good—in the modern world that is what sells. Your first kiss. Yes, I like that; yes, that would do. My pen is poised. Tell me, paint the scene.

You look up. You prepare to speak. And here we go:

It was the middle of a surprisingly hot English summer; and you were beneath the shade of a mulberry tree. (Mulberry is good. It has a softness ripe for the creation of romantic metaphor.)

No?

You were indoors, lying on a bed, far, far from the world beyond the room. That we can also work in. You had been there for long? Hours, perhaps? Days, you say? Time feels long indeed to those who love. Continue.

It was summer, and outside there were bees in the borders of the walled garden high on the hill. (Sadly not an

Elizabethan manor, but a monumental house nonetheless. Victorian. Sandstone. Designed for women in bonnets and uniforms to glide silently along corridors.) The orangery (you say) was long deserted, but the lawns roamed far, with paths by all those borders and more paths by the dilapidated tennis court. I imagine no-one played on this July afternoon? No-one? I had thought as much. And so you lay, eyes closed, body still, waiting.

Had your eyes been open, they would have looked past the ceiling with its ancient white paint melted unevenly into off-white, its cornice mutilated when the room was divided after a century of intact glory, a crack which you will notice later scrawled in Hebrew across one corner. Even with eyes open the curtains at the window, rustling in the breeze, would have blocked your view. Your languorous limbs sank into the mattress, unmoved for many hours. White sheets covered your body, holding off the pollen-laden breeze. The heat, the heat.

So tell me, my dear, tell me about the man for whose kiss you are waiting. His antecedents, accomplishments, profession and name. Describe him for me. You say there is little that you can tell. You pause, I encourage you, you begin to speak. So: he is not dark-haired and handsome in the cliché of fairy tales, but blond, shortish, tanned, with a loose-limbed stride. You met him in the evening among drinks and people and cigarette smoke. He, like you, was alone. He was energetic, was wide-shouldered, was talkative, with a fast smile; but for all that you saw that his soul was empty, that he was not yet loved. He is coming today because he loves you. Because he has singled out your soul to be his love. And you will be kissed for the first time, though you do not yet know it.

Despite the heat there are voices now in the garden.

Adults talking quietly, conserving their energy with the strength of those who have forgotten why they would sweat and play. Drifting past the trees and through the window and the curtains they arrive like flotsam on the surface of your mind, pushed one way and another as the leaves rustle and in the distance a church bell tolls out the long afternoon. And now children are calling, rushing between the roses, down the paths to the orangery, and round the tennis courts, stooping for a wizened ball and losing it again in the undergrowth where the hill steepens and drops away to a view of tiled roofs.

And now he is coming. His footsteps are on the boards of the corridor, and he is outside the door, crossing the room, and he is seated on your bed. He pauses, and then, tentatively, he takes your left hand in both of his.

You lie on your bed. For a moment he sits, watching you breathe. Then he draws in his own breath, and, less tentative now, he shuffles himself so your heavy arm bends to his hands and he can sit in comfort. Now he begins to talk. It's a beautiful day outside today. Let him tell you: he woke early, and ran through the quiet streets and down to the river. (His voice is quick, tripping over its words.) Mist rose from the water, moorhens were busy at their nests, and the sun threw the reeds horizontally like spears. A brisk four miles out and back; that was what he needed to begin the day (that—you remember now—is how his day begins). Then it was cool, but now it is hot, and in his formal long-sleeved shirt he is hotter. Your hand, he tells you, is cool between his. (He pauses; the gap is a pause too long.) Then: it's Sunday, he reminds you, but not quite a day of rest. (He feels guilt that all days are ones of rest for you.) He did the list of tasks he had set out to do. Admin, laundry, clearing up the flat. Boring, he says, but necessary, and you do not reply. That was it really; he hopped on his bike and here he is. He has been talking to you and you have not heard him.

Now he greets you by name, stroking the back of your hand. Some might say he is pleading. Listen to him, *listen*. Can you now remember what he said then? You are silent. And he is now silent, stroking your hand. Is there really nothing to say?

Down in the town a bell strikes the hour; briefly its beat shapes the air.

He is uneasy. He shifts on the bed, manoeuvring your elbow, arm, wrist and hand to lie straight on the sheet, and he looks at them—he does not look at your face. He feels he has been irresponsible, that somehow he has failed you, yet how was he to know?

Now he has to leave. He has friends coming for drinks and dinner and first he needs to shop. He does not say he is already late; he does not tell you that you will be with friends again soon; he does not know whether you even have friends. Leaving your arm on the sheet, this shortish man stands to his full height and turns for the door. Then, indecisive, he turns back, takes a pace to the bed, rocks on the balls of his feet, and leans in sympathy to kiss your dry lips. And you do not notice it. But in time you will look back, searching for your youth, and this will have been your first kiss.

There are voices in the corridor, then his footsteps retreat. Someone enters, talks and goes away. You lie still, and beyond the room the day moves slowly on.

I pause. I purse my lips.

Well, my dear, you have played an elegant trick. You promised to tell me about your first kiss and, yes, to the letter, you've fulfilled that task. But you know as well as I that what you have given me is nothing. All that you have told me here I already know. I know, to put it bluntly, that you're in the hospital, know you are not yet quite aware of that, know that you are afraid.

What you don't know is that I know more. Yes, my dear, no need for shock. This story is not just yours to tell: we agreed to thrash out how much editorial control you have, but, for the record, there are parts which I will add. The view from this chair, my perspective, as it were. And those voices that came when he left the room, that was not the nurses, that was me. You take me for a fool, but I was (in advance) protecting my investment of effort and time. From outside your room I saw him emerge.

Peter talked more to me than he did to you.

You want to know? (I see alarm on your face.) Alright, I'm prepared this time to tell.

He came out of your room, closed the door behind him, and as his head went down his footstep slowed and he sighed a deep sigh which, passing by, was a sign I just happened to hear. He was disorientated, confused, and, as I say, I happened to be passing by, so I offered him a cup of tea. He looked at me and he blinked, and in that moment I believe my graciousness awakened in him a hallowed image: in me he saw his velvet-dressed mother pouring tea on her bridge afternoons, with the chocolate labrador by the fire in the drawing room, the neat stacks of cards on the green baize, and, back-stage in the kitchen, the piles of crusts cut sharply off the tidy sandwiches. And so, pulled in a way that maybe even he did not wholly understand, he said, 'What? Tea? Yes. Please'.

And I said, 'Come.'

He looked surprised as I took his arm but he let me lead him down the high-ceilinged corridor and into the drawing room at the end. Though my poor fingers were thin against his crisp, striped cotton sleeve, with my rings and his cufflinks we made an elegant pair. But then the sight that greeted us there, —O my darling, my darling—I swallowed hard and I smiled, but truly I tell you I struggled to hold onto my grace.

Hear this: I had laid out tea over the un-stacked tables which were placed, just so, by the cosiest armchairs, had arranged the cake and sandwiches on platters, had added water to the tea leaves. But in the few minutes I had been away (just in the corridor, just passing by) one of those scruffy, stubbly men had come in, and with him a dirty woman with her hair all over and in her pyjamas and not even a shred of make-up and now they were there, and now the fat television I'd shrouded in the corner was uncovered and shouting out quiz questions (a bed-sheet, the indignity, beside it on the floor). The shame, the shame! I apologised of course, patting always at his arm, but those people caused something to change in him, in your lovely boy, caused prickles to grow in his eyes and all of a sudden he began to pull back. Not from me, you hear, but from them as they and the quiz show host shouted back and forth.

Still, we had tea together, he and I. My hands shook a little (an effect of the pills) but I poured out the cup, and how would he like it, a slice of cake with that, won't you please? In that rowdiness he could hardly hear me speak, yet slowly, slowly he began to settle again, and eventually he smiled back down at my hand, put out his hand, patted mine . So I was the one before whom his confusion poured out. I asked a few questions, of course, about him, you, how you met. I said the party sounded nice, that it was kind of him to walk you home. I reassured him, *of course,* that you'll be OK, that all of this is treatable, that you'll wake up soon, recognise him, respond to his love. And he stuttered a little, said that you were just a friend, no, just that party, and then for coffee once or twice, mumbled that for some reason after all this time you had come to him and he'd just tried to do his best. I placed my hand on his at that, and he blushed. Then he looked up at me, and blushed deeper, said he'd never been somewhere like this before, said I was so kind.

Oh, we talked for a while. He grew up in Canada, did you know? His family is there still. A brave lad, I thought, crossing the world like that—and I told him so, making him blush, the pink showing through the tan of his cheeks. It was for a scholarship, he said. Oxford. (I was quietly impressed.) And now he's in the law, and nearly qualified, living up here in his own place on the north side of town. I thought of him in court with a gavel and in one of those wigs and we smiled together over the idea. Ever the gentleman he asked too about me: call me 'Iris' I said to him, 'but of course really it's Lady Buchanan; the honour comes from my husband's side.' He looked surprised at that and looked down again at my hand. It was my ring he was looking at; people always do.

'For sorrow,' I told him. 'A pearl for sorrow.' And the diamonds around it were meant to be for joy.

As you can tell, we were companionable together; and conversation was easier now that the ugly pair across the room had slumped into silence behind the settee. (The television is something I have grown to ignore; it is never quiet here, my love, I can never rest.) I was only sorry he could not tell me more about you—at least, he claimed he had no more to tell. But maybe his reticence was just flirtation. He did not, for example, say he had come from kissing you; *you* have just added that piece to my collage. You can see why, we two having grown already so close, he would not want to reveal that to me.

But maybe it was just that we ran out of time. For he had barely had the chance to sip at his tea, poor man, when one of those nurses came roaring in and looked round the room and stopped and stared at us there.

'This is Peter,' I told her. 'He and I are having tea. No need to worry, nothing to do'. But the damage was already done and, torn from our tête-à-tête, he was standing up and smoothing his hands down his trouser creases.

'I'm so sorry,' I heard her say as she drove him out of the room. 'She's harmless, but she does tend to catch people up.'

And that whispering bustling witch dragged him away and out of sight. So I sat, and I finished drinking my tea, alone. I didn't cry at her insults. No, I tell you, I did not cry. No, I turned my back on the television and thought of that darling boy.

You also are unmoving.

Behind your eyelids the room is dark, what remains of the day lying still on the surface of high tide. There is no calling from the world beyond the room. Footsteps enter, pause, leave. Footsteps return. They are noisy this time, with the uneven clatter of several shoes on wood at once. Part of the doctor almost has a voice. He explains they need to test more of your blood. He needs your permission for the sample. He is trying to sound serious, to sound stern. He waits. They all wait. Then in the distance someone takes your wrist and rolls it outwards so the pale crook of your arm is opened. You do not feel the needle go in. The low hum of voices slops against the shore. The waves and tide are held in stillness by the moon.

II

My dear, my dear, please don't cry like that. Please. Here, take a tissue. Do tell me what it is. Here, take it. That's better. Now go on. (Deep breath. Yours and mine.) You say that I've got it completely wrong. Your breath stutters and it gulps. You say that Peter is not in love. Not in love at all with me or with you. (Maybe I should have been more careful, in telling you all that I heard.) You say it isn't like that at all. You take another deep breath, and look at me, and say that we need to start again.

I disagree. And not just because I'm invested here already. Listen: I hear what you say. That you are not quite yourself at the moment; that love may be a complexity too far right now. I get that you're confused. That you're shying away from commitment. But I know what I saw in him as well. I am prepared to admit to an over-estimate of the current strength of his feeling for me—sad to say, but he is, after all, your age and not mine. (You will learn that in the afternoons I can get carried away. It comes on at eighteen minutes past four. That is what the official report said. That is what they tell me, and it is good to be exact. Otherwise, even in my clearer moments, I would not understand.) As far as his love for you is concerned, though, I am even more sure than I was. The kiss was not the kiss I was expecting. But there is love here. Let me set out my stall:

There is love here, but it's not a happy love. I see that now in your eyes. (You look up from your hands to my face.) And he is not happy either. You're surprised? You nod, hesitantly. You hadn't thought about that? Don't cry. You are mutually unhappy. But that in itself need not be a problem. Let's face it, happiness is usually boring. This way you both have something interesting to say. So, no need to go back to the blank page quite yet. Though not Elizabethan, we have an orangery and gardens; they are ripe for our setting, and they will do tragedy just as well as romance.

Let's just think about this for a minute. I can picture how poor Peter's story will work: he will be in love with you though he is not yet sure of it. (He will also be torn by affection for me. He will be tossed on a tempestuous sea, will undergo a spiritual transformation, will reach a qualified fulfilment of his desire or will end the tale sitting in the stillness, alone.) Yes, Peter is clear; there I know what to say. But when it comes to you I'm afraid that I'm lost. What sort of story do you want to tell? What do you want me to help you tell? Do you yearn towards him? Will you ultimately accept his love? So far, I'm afraid, it's all too oblique. It's lacking punch. Not going anywhere. We can do something about all of that; as I said, I'm open to something more explicit. But you do have to provide the material. You shake your head—you're not ready for that? Fine. I can see we still need to build that deeper trust. Then help me at least to move on from where we are. My pen awaits your orders.

You're hesitating. Have a sip of water from that flimsy plastic cup. Take a deep breath. Go on, tell me. I'm on your side. You can trust me. This is for you.

Then: Peter has left your room, you say. You have moved (and that's a good sign). Or at the least someone has turned you. (Carry on. Here, take another tissue. There's a bin under the table, just by your right foot.) Now, you remember, you are faced to the wall, one arm pushed out to support your shoulders, its hand mid-way between your eyes and the plaster, your knees gently bent so your weight curves forward under the sheets. In the world outside the sun is shining, the breeze soft, the warm heat of morning or afternoon playing through the window. There are people on the paths through the window. Real people, pointing at the borders and bending ostentatiously to sniff the bright colours; people who know the flowers' names, and whose shoes scuff the gravel as they walk.

You pause. But this scene is good, I tell you. Hold this scene and I will paint in its detail, stroke by stroke. Watch me here: I'm in my element, and I can really make this sing.

I see you lying here like a second Titian Venus. The picture he never drew from behind, with sunlight falling on a rounded head of dull gold hair, a long back, your buttocks, legs, and heels. I agree with you now that we were wrong to start where we did. You were right to hold back. Even in memory you were not waiting in a suspension of bliss for your lover; Venus does not wait around for lovers to come to her bed. Locked in this room you are a self-contained world, and those people are the right backdrop, the crowd in the street outside.

Behind this window on this summer afternoon, with the bells warmly tolling, Venus is luxuriating. Her shape is a shape which has led the wanton down through centuries in a glory of nakedness. From behind, though, the rounded curves of hip, thigh and calf are whitely exposed to a prying world. She cannot relish being the object of voyeurism from this angle. Here she is unprotected by the complicity of her usual challenging gaze. She is weaker. We must only imagine that her hand still plays with slick abandon in her now-secret hair.

What do you think? I like that. I think it works. A

recognisable image transmuted to fit the tremble I can hear in your voice. It gives the story an artistic shape. And yes, my dear, I still hear you tremble, and, yes, your face is blotched. You refuse to tell me anything, you refuse to answer my questions, but I think you can remember. And so we go on:

Your hair is spread across your pillow and shoulders. It is matted like long-fibred felt. But still such golden hair cannot be that of a dying lady. The sun on your back is holding alive the thinned blood in your veins. You do not yet feel any warmth, but you are certainly not dead.

You are certainly not dead. You are beginning to know that. Evidence of the world has risen on the tide, and is pushing at the shore. Though unseen, the mist is lifting in gentle spirals from the water. And now your eyes are open.

There is a shadow on the wall beyond your hand. It has fluctuating edges, grey on what your mind's eye sees as a wall of blotting whiteness. (The wall is in fact the pale colour of dirtied parchment and beyond the field of your gaze is a poster of some of Van Gogh's sunflowers, mustard yellow cheaply framed in lurid green plastic. But let's gloss over that. For now it's off the edge of the scene; it will be some time before you see it. By that time, frankly, I'd have hoped to have got rid of it.)

Twenty centimetres from your eyes the shadow is crawling right to left across the wall. Your eyes are watching it, are locked on its movement like an enthralled young child with a shadow puppet butterfly. It coalesced from nothing and grew into relief, darker against the paler wall. At first it was elongated, thinner, the gentle slope up the right side a barely inclined plane. But it crawls. And as it crawls its shape changes. Your eyes track it.

Out in the world is a sense of time: there is a regularity

in the ringing of the bells, and less frequently in the sounds of crockery and glass; in a room down the corridor there is a television permanently on, the screen jogging memories with a co-ordinated schedule of colour, movement and chatter; an elegant lady with a large pearl ring and perfectly coiffured dove-grey hair sits and serenely hears its offerings come and go. The sun rises, and then it sets. (And when it sets there come the nights when other people's screams are placed in relief by the dark.)

You lie, unmoving. The world turns around you. Something within you is strained to hear its whisper.

Now the shadow is more bunched, a caterpillar primed for its next slide forwards, each step down the left steeper, camouflaging fewer of the fossilised particles of dust caught years ago in the drying surface of the paint. Each of those casts its own shadow. Tiny greyed footprints across the wall, spotted, scattered, each tethered tightly to its own particle. But look, within that narrow circumference they too crawl.

Voices float in fragments in the corridor.

Footsteps come and go on the wooden floor.

This time they do not ask you about the needle. You have retreated so far you do not feel its repeated prick and pull as they search for a vein. And when the footsteps have gone away the shadow is longer again, is spreading and becoming the wall. Or the wall is being absorbed into your mind.

How many people have lain here and watched this wall grow old? Think about it.

Think harder.

The wall has become its own shadow and your eyes are locked on where the earlier shadow came to rest.

III

Let me tell you what I have learned:

Peter opened his door to an unexpected mid-afternoon knock and he found you on the step. After all those weeks it took him a moment to recognise your face; cleaned of make-up your skin was chalk-pale and your dirty hair was pulled straight back from your forehead. Then you looked up, mute, and, horror-struck, all he could do was take your arm and bring you inside. Whatever he did, whatever he asked, you said nothing—as though the energy that led you to his door and onto the chair in his hall was already borrowed beyond your due. The sweet tea he made sat chilling at your feet. When despite the heat you shivered he fetched the duvet from his single bed and tucked it over your lap, but it made no difference, and after a full two hours he gave in to his foreboding and called for an ambulance. You were shaking with tears; but said nothing.

The paramedic ran a series of checks: your pulse, blood pressure, temperature; and a light shone into the back of your eyes. He saw nothing. Your reflexes kicked up at him automatically as though your nerves were straining to emerge but something had stolen the rest of your soul. You made no response to weight on your sternum, no response to the pressure on the beds of your fingernails which nearly made Peter scream.

From A&E it took them four hours to get the blood tests back and then to confirm a bed. Then Peter helped them as they put their hands under your arms and legs and pulled, and your muscles half-contracted and you went with them into the taxi. Peter accompanied you to the other hospital, saw you admitted beyond the locked doors, and though protesting bare acquaintance signed the forms on your behalf. After that he sat at a corner table in the nearest pub, stared at the wall and got very drunk.

Neither he nor you will ever remember the hours that followed him bringing you here.

But now it is different. Now we are past that stage. Now you will both begin to tell.

See:

Your hand has a beauty you have never seen before. Your brain is astonished by its novelty. Close enough for your eyes to focus without effort, it rises from the knobble on your wrist to the peak of your middle finger knuckle, and falls joint by cantilevered joint to where your smooth nails nestle in the white of the sheets. Its hairs are blond; white gold where the light gives its reflection to each one in turn. They are uneven, some almost upright in spindly disorder, others around and below forming the nap of a sparse but rich velvet. Longer on the back of your hand, they grow short and tidy in the swelling plains which run between your knuckles. Beneath them travel underground rivers, dark webbed veins following an indirect pattern across the plain. In the shadow of your wrist are your exposed tendons, archaeological in a purpose which is lost to you. One is pulsing lightly. Watch it. Watch it and you will see. You see. You believe you feel the bones beneath the skin, the levers designed to pull awake the translucent folds between thumb and first finger, now crumpled and shadowed like a discarded fan.

Your right hand is the world to you. No tall ships and tempests, but a clean lunar landscape, fresh in the light of a new-born sun.

(Or like Michelangelo's anatomical drawings, perhaps,

all levers and straight lines but drawn with the filigree delicacy of true devotion. A human architecture.)

You watch it.

Is it yours? The longer you look the further it is from you. Though not bloodless, it is pale. Hairs, veins and bones hold still. Only the shadow behind it moves. Your mind remembers it must advance out towards your hand, that there is a connection to be made, a transferred ache which is followed by movement, that this is what it is for. But your mind and your hand are made of different materials. Your thought slips, frictionless, over and through your body, a jellyfish shimmer down and back. As it passes no molecules vibrate and fire. You should be afraid. You have been still for so long that no memory remains of the feeling of anything brushing your nerves. You see the stiffness in your sheets. The stiffness touches your fingers, but unless the fingers can move you will not feel it. The only feeling is in movement; that is why the dead do not feel. This thought settles your mind. Your hand retreats to nothingness.

And so.

Then:

Someone has placed a different hand on your shoulder. You felt its arrival. Now its heavy warmth is raising a dew beneath the sheet. It trickles into the sweetish smell your immobility in the heat has drawn around you, thread by thread like a silk cocoon. The breeze is not strong enough for you yet to have noticed it.

Peter has gritted his teeth against it, and is talking—has been talking for some time. He has nothing to say. The weather again is beautiful today. He walked up the hill from his flat rather than cycling – too hot to cycle, and anyway there's a problem with the brakes which needs fixing. He wouldn't fancy going downhill again with them the way they are. They have started juddering for some reason. Maybe something got misaligned when he bashed it on a bollard the other day. (His talk is a presence and your brain begins to tune in and out.) Today's a pretty busy day so he's afraid he can't stay long. Has to get some work done this afternoon, loads of things to do.

He stops and he wonders what it really is that he needs to do. He has nothing lined up in his memory. He stutters to a halt. For a moment he just sits there. His hand is on your shoulder, your smell is in his nostrils.

Then, breaking the silence: 'I saw that woman Iris again this morning. The one with the purple shirt and that huge pearl ring. You'll see her a lot when you're out of bed. She said hello, said to say hello to you, said she hopes you are doing OK.'

He passes on my message as though it is normal to pass on the greetings of those who have never met. Then he pauses, not knowing where to go next. Then,—and in honour I record what I heard—then, 'Crazy woman,' he says, and pats your hand. 'Thought she was some sort of greeter when she first ambushed me in the corridor. Like those people in the foyers of five star hotels. I must have been a bit confused. She goes and pours me tea like in a period drama. On and on she went about how she's Lady Buchanan, talking to me like a long-lost son.'

He pauses. He does not know how confused his mind has become, does not know what he should have expected here; how it should have been different from how it has been. (Does not know how inappropriately he maligns my care.) He adds, as though someone is listening again (as though he has seen me trembling with my ear to the door): 'really sad to see someone who's fallen apart like that.'

He pauses again, and in his silence he wonders what he is doing here. It occurs to him that his position is unfair, that he's got to the point where he wants something back. On the flimsiest of acquaintances he has brought you here, visited you, now is racking his brains for kind thoughts to make your life more gentle, yet all he does is merely swallowed up into the broiling summer room. Suddenly he is angry at what is going on. He wants to grasp and shake your shoulder, to cause you a pain which will cut right through to wherever you are, even just for a moment. To force you, wherever you are, to acknowledge him, to feel. Alarmed at his impulse, he pulls his hand away, wipes it dry on his jeans, and stops talking.

For a moment he too is still and his mind comes to a halt. Then he rouses himself. He tells himself that he has done enough, that now is the time for him to leave you to your fate, but though inwardly he can say the words, when he looks down at your face he knows this is not yet the end; he cannot yet dissociate himself from your presence in this room. (If he watches closely enough then he can see your nostrils breathe.) He opens his mouth to speak, then closes it again.

A nurse enters. 'Any signs of movement?'

'No, nothing so far'. As though he is your keeper, the one they come to to know.

She says, 'We're going to need to get her on a drip,' and he hears her leave the room.

Outside, the breeze is transporting voices. A child is visiting its mother, and does not understand why she does not move or speak. The child begins to cry.

Yes.

Before all of this you dreamed of a white room. That was all. It had no size or shape, no shadows or dust in the corners. The paint had never faded to parchment. No-one had lived there. It had neither history nor future. It had no temperature. It was empty. Now you do not know how you knew it was a room. (Modern art, perhaps. A room which is whiteness alone, a stasis of blotting nothingness held isolated from the world. Am I right? If you agree then we should use that image. It's one that people will understand. Are you listening to me? Listen to me, I understand how your mind works. Listen. Why will you not hear?) Someone once suggested you should create it in physical reality. But it could not be created. And there was no need.

You took yourself into it. Though your eyes were still open you switched off one by one the nerves that gave you both soul and body. Your limbs moved away from your mind. You were spread. You could not move, or speak, or feel. Sitting or lying in real rooms with real people you disappeared from yourself. They rushed around you. Listen to me. What's wrong? Tell me what's wrong. Listen to me. You saw your room, close enough that you did not need to yearn for it. You rested. You were there for hours.

But through that time something stayed alive. You always returned. You never knew how long had passed, but at the right moment the right chemical released itself into your blood and you came back. The room remained but you saw the rest of the world. You cannot remember those shifts back, but they must have happened because you always carried on living. Moving backwards and forwards was normal to you, a familiar commute; your room was your natural home.

Right now you are passing through the room on your way back to the world. It is still a stasis of white. (Platonic white?) But from this angle it is different, something is unfamiliar. The sense of difference intrigues your brain, begins to tip it from neutrality to concentration. Something hardens and focuses, and then a muscle contracts. The room is different. It is no longer wholly empty. Looking from here there may be a window on the other side. You do not see it, but you hear the voices. People are speaking in words.

You blink.

A pause.

You blink again. You feel your eyelids bring themselves down to form a locked-tight seal on the perfectly-shaped curve below. Then they spring instantly open again as though open were their natural state. The voices are speaking in a language you know.

They are speaking. They are. They.

(No - no! Don't stop. Please don't stop. We were getting on so well. We really were. For once I felt some movement, some hope. I was beginning to see how it would all pan out. Please don't stop. 'They are speaking'. Go on. Tell me.)

They are.

But there is no window. The room is heavy and white.

IV

The room is heavy and it is white, but now a voice says it is morning and you believe it. For days you have been lying here, not certainly not dead. And now you are here. You have woken up. You have seen the shadow, seen your hand, and now finally you have remembered. You have remembered that you want to die.

They have told you it is morning, and you close your eyes against its brightness. You close them and you look for your room. For the first time since you arrived you are afraid. You cannot see the room. It is suddenly only a memory, and without it you cannot feel nothing, without it you need more than ever to die. But your body is awakening. Your eyes want to open; your bones are beginning to ache. You have been lying so still for so long that you have felt nothing, you have forgotten how to feel. But now your body is remembering.

There is a pain deep in your right hip. It began just before they told you it was morning, and without the whiteness it is insistent. It is spreading like the fear of cancer down your thigh to where your knee now feels a scratchy sheet on the mattress, and up to your shoulder which is too hot where your hair is clumped against it. Something is alive like caffeine in your veins.

You need to turn over.

For the first time you know there is a brightness in the day. That is why you have remembered you want to die.

You need to turn over.

(You are not yet surprised by your need.)

Your left hand finds it can press down on the bed, and

that as you straighten your arm it makes your shoulders turn and your torso twist. You open your eyes and see the ceiling. You blink. The pain in your hip is already lessened. Your head aches with sudden movement. You wait.

You are afraid that they will notice—as though turning is an admission that you have failed not only to die, but even to stay beyond the world where you had no mind and felt no need. You are guilty of having turned.

You are guilty. But without noticing it you have pulled up your knees, disturbing the rippled sheet, and twisted them, so now your torso turns the opposite way, and your eyes are almost towards the window.

It is sunny: sunny.

And, O my darling, my darling, may I speak for one minute? May I interrupt? I need to say that I was hoping this was coming. Waiting, and hoping, and then longing for it, as much for you as for myself. And for Peter as well. Poor Peter, who has visited and sat with you every day, buoyed only by the dedication of a lover for his love. Maybe he should not love you, but he truly does, and until now you have not repaid him. But now you can!

Now you see the sun, bright and fearless! Its presence here is gentle, but it burns with strength. Its essence is strength. (You see that Venus was the right image for you, Venus and her long, golden hair?) I'm seeing in you now what I always said was there: I'm seeing love, life, strength and hope; I'm absorbing it with all my heart. He loves you, and you can now love him. Today you can respond when he visits. The world once again can begin to turn.

There are roses, and bees, and still a breeze, nay, a zephyr, which shifts the shadows as they take their gradual journey across the cricket-green lawn. (The beauty of this setting has not deserted you as you lay and deserted it.)

The birds sing.

He loves you.

And you're looking up. (I must say that I'm rather pleased with myself.) But, no—I see your look. What? Why do you hate me? Don't you dare to deny it; in that glance upwards there was nothing but hate. Why? I have done nothing to deserve it. I am trying, only trying, to tell your story, to help you tell your story to yourself (and for him). Your eyes are dead now, but I saw it happen. I saw your hatred. It is something you cannot deny.

Why would you hate me? I am telling the truth. Your truth. You have finally turned and seen the sun, and now there's a chance your silence, your selfish, cold, silence, will break and you will give that man the start of the response he needs. Had you even thought to consider what he needs? No? I knew it. I was being kind, dressing up my response in happiness for you. But now you've come clean, and so, frankly, will I. He is doing all that he can for you, and you lie and you wait without even the acknowledgement a rejection of him would give. And I don't care if you cry. I don't, and I won't. Cry. Go on. Cry.

Cry, you fool. It is right that you should. You are wasting his life as well as your own.

Yes: your eyes now are dead to the sun. You do not need to close them against it. All your energy has been used in that one guilt-ridden turn. Your room is hovering almost in reach, close enough that you need only reach out for its touch.

You lie there, still, feeling nothing.

You lie.

But when you wake you are waiting for him. Today. Your newly acquired sense of time knows there is a rhythm to the day, and that now it is the afternoon he will come to you. They told you it was morning, and you turned and slept and so it must be soon that he will come. Lying still beneath your sheets you are finally waiting.

As you wait, something is twisting deep inside your body. It started after you turned, and it is linked to the ache in your head, to the dryness in your throat, to the sheets of loose dead skin in your mouth, and to the weakness which allows you to lie for hours without the shadow of movement beyond the hyphenated twitch of your pulse in your jaw. It beats, it beats, but you do not move. You are staring towards the ceiling. Its plaster is cracked, and there is a fly between you and it. Your eyes try to focus on one and then on the other. The fly is moving, is darting in spirals with a faint buzz which is not the whine of a mosquito stepping back and forth over the edge of consciousness. This buzz is here, quiet but insistent. You hear, but the effort of rolling your eyes with it is too much, so you watch the crack. Easier, still.

And when you hear the steps outside you close your eyes. You are surprised by the instinctive movement, by its automatic artfulness. 'A cry for help'. That was the phrase you heard them say in the first words you heard. You are guilty of crying for help. Closing your eyes locks shame inside you.

But now Peter is here and for the first time you know you are sure of it. He is sitting on your bed, and taking your hand, as he has done every day since first you were here. Today his hands around yours are warm, and his words are directed at you. You do not want to feel him and hear him, but since your bones first ached your senses have become alive. This time his pleading may have an effect.

'Darling, listen to me.' (The 'darling' is medicinal. They are worried that you are afraid. They have asked him to comfort you.)

'Listen. No-one is going to hurt you. No-one is going to take you away. But we need you to drink something.' He holds back from mentioning the threat of the drip. (He need not bother; you heard and ignored that yesterday while the afternoon needle was in your arm. There still was no pain as they prodded and poked in the bruises for a vein, but something of what you heard lodged firm in your brain.)

'Darling?'

Your head hurts with the strain of focusing behind his voice, on the door to the whiteness you trust. You can still hear the fly. And Peter is rubbing your hands gently, as though you are out cold and slowly drawing away. You open your eyes.

You open them, and you see his face, close to yours and full of pity. He smiles. 'Well done, my love, I know how hard that was for you.' The tears are in his eyes and not in yours. He is still rubbing your hands. You do not see the fly. You watch the crack.

You are still, but against all his expectation Peter is heroically overjoyed. After days of purposeless visiting he is the one to touch you and bring you back towards the world. Out of illness and compassion has been created an exclusive relationship, and that has given him both serenity and pride. Lifted wholly out of time he is supremely content. In his rhythmically rubbing hands he is holding a moment he will never forget. (The two of you are closer now than you will ever be again. Wait. Hold that still. Tread gently on the lawns, touch your cutlery silently to your plate. Wait. Wait. Be gentle. Be silent.

But it has gone.)

Peter is forcing his breathing to slow, forcing himself

to hold his smile. He has awoken to the knowledge that this uniquely pure moment has a simpler purpose: it is medically precious. That it could tip in his suddenly dry hands to normality or inhumane efficiency. He cannot bear the thought of the drip, the condoned torture of electrotherapy, the gloved hands throwing you instantly and without memory into bare electric light. Tipped out of serenity he is afraid.

'We need you to drink something.'

You have not forgotten. You will never forget. The words will always be there, calcified into your bones, firing your reflexes whenever you are sad for the rest of your life. You have not forgotten, so it is right that they are the first words you say:

'I want to die.'

Your voice is dry with lack of use, but it has worked to contact the world. You do not say it again. Already you have made a link which was not there before. Your words are one step further from fulfilment.

Peter knows it. The link is almost nothing, but tangible to both your senses. A thread of scent on the air. Delicate beauty for him, and something as strong as fear for you. He is still holding this moment, holding it gently, but in sudden terror that he has nothing to say. He knows as you do that there is no answer to your desire. It is absolute as his is not. It can have no answer, so he hesitates, and as he does you are drifting away from him.

Then: 'Darling, you can't die here. No-one here will let you die.'

'I want to die.' The thread is strengthened. Neither of you hears the trolley as it moves along the corridor. You are struggling with logic. He waits. Now he can afford to wait.

'I can't drink something. If I drink I won't die.'

This is new, not a reflex repetition. You have searched for and found a new logical path. It is the first new thought you have had in all the time since he brought you here, and Peter is horrified by its—by your—tenacity, by the fact that you have come so close to death and it has not revolted you. (It will be some time before you know how close it was you came. No-one will tell you until they are sure the conscious temptation has gone.) He is still rubbing, rubbing.

'You're wrong. They won't let you. It would take at least six months for you to die here'. The number is arbitrary, but then his mind counts out to January. Your mind also counts, more slowly. Six is an eternity away.

'Here, drink this,' and his timing is perfect. He has caught you wounded by fear and alone, stunned by time which you didn't know existed until this morning. He has tempted you and you drink. And now you are crying and he is rocking your wounds in his arms. He has gained you a day's respite, and he also is weeping with exhaustion and relief.

There is nothing left to say.

And so Peter has gone, but your salt-wounded eyes are still open. You can see out of the window, can see the tops of trees, and the sky. (It is a blue so warm you should reach out to stroke it). You see the world again, and its mode is wrong. It is not your own, but now you will not even die.

V

Before you came here you lived in a world of self-hatred and shame. Now it is in remnants, purged to the thinness of dry-frozen tissue-paper then blown apart in a gusty wind. Semi-transparent, it crackles insubstantially around you. If your hair were clean it would be alive with static. With the destruction of your world your room has also gone. The white is cracked and scrawled upon. You are not nowhere, you are here.

You now smell your own smell, not acrid but sweet, organic without being fresh.

You are blinking with eyes crusted by their own excretions.

Your knees are on the boards in the corridor, largely facing forwards. Your hands, in loose fists, are both on one wall. They snag on the roughness of paint that was dusty when it dried.

(No-one would draw this, let us be clear. The aesthetics are purely those of disgust. You may have risen, but not to new life.)

The distance to the end of the corridor is infinite. People pass. Probably they stare. You are clothed. Someone would have stopped you if you were not. People pass, and they fade. You have been here for an hour. More. Almost crawling. Not quite. This is progress.

You move a hand crab-wise along the wall then shuffle a knee. Slowly your weight is transferred forward. All of your life is wrapped up in this movement.

You will not eat, but they want you in the dining room for lunch. As though you were a child to be trained.

Presence at meals is a step towards civilisation, a gesture towards damask napkins, heavy silver cutlery and waiters who stand to push your chair in as you sit. But lunch is long over, so no-one is quite sure why you are still here. Still moving, if not yet with the will of the dogged.

You move. Slowly. One hand, then the other. One knee. The other. Time passes, but they have not forgotten you. They tell each other this is good.

But it is not enough. And so someone has discovered that pulling at your arms can make you stand and be leaned against the wall. And now having done that with effort they too give in. You lean. They stand. They wait. And then the pretence that you might eat is over.

They turn you round.

(Interesting, isn't it, that their tenses are wrong. By three in the afternoon you were still there moving forward in the corridor because they hoped you might eat at a time long gone. As though your past is still in front of you, in denial of the truth that you have lost what might have been.)

They turn you, and they take your arms, talking softly and pulling you forwards so it is your feet which now shuffle and not your knees. They take you back, pull down the sheets they have changed, and watch as you pull them up to your neck and close your eyes. They hope you sleep.

You sleep.

They sign out at the end of their shifts.

And all of the time Peter has been with you, watching, talking, lending you his arm. He has affected nonchalance in banter with the nurses. His throat has swelled with pity which made him reach out and touch you. Funny you will never be sure he was here. Odd that you'll never quite know.

VI

We should take a break, time out, a moment to reflect. Maybe I owe you an apology, maybe not. But either way I'm confused. (There, I've said it; I'm clean.) They say this is progress, and it is, I know, but it stops me in my tracks, it jerks at the cords of both my heart and my mind. I know what you are thinking. No, really, I do. You find me superficial, foolish, self-dramatising, even cruel. And, above all, wrong. (I see all of that in your eyes.) But I'm none of those things. Really not. I'm confused, and below that I'm torn and hurt. Despite all the pills that they make me take, I too bleed when I see your blotched face, your dull eyes, your hunched shoulders, your stare. I empathise with your pain. I do; I have an ache in my forehead which is new to me, and my back is tensed up as it has not been for years. I have empathy. But also I care deeply for the aesthetics of your tale. In aesthetics, that is where my confusion lies. Think back, take a turn through the scenes we've drawn together since we agreed upon our pact: lying in your curtained bed high on the hill you were Sleeping Beauty; on your side once the curtains were parted and crowds meandered in the distance beyond the window you really did have potential for Titian's Venus. The shapes and the settings were right, though your hair did not shine as I knew that it could. Despite it all you were ethereal, lovely, translucent, true. But now you are dirty. It pains me. I still don't want to sell this. We don't want to sell this. But all the same beauty matters, and suddenly I find none of it here.

Why are you surprised? Beauty does matter. And where

we are now is worse than I've admitted. Out of pity I'm holding myself back. Do you want to hear? You claim you want to hear. Here it is, the truth: I'm repulsed. You repulse me. I can't help it; this is the truth.

Look at yourself now. See yourself as I see you, my senses all recoiling despite myself: the smell, the crusted eyes, the crawling mess with dirty hair. My horror has not even the purity of being awestruck. There is no awe here. And that response is caused by you, is all the world sees of you, and I hate it. Hate it. I can barely bear to look.

Because all I know is the romantic, so there is nothing I can do to get your story right. I know, my dear, that I am failing you, that my whole mode is wrong for what you want to say. My endgame is pearlescent castles on symmetrical hills, with a stream (bordered by flowers) laughing to the sea, and you with Peter eating plums on the bank. Or a boy with his pipes on the chalk downs, and you stepping towards him across soft, flared grass. Or the luxury of silks in a room lit by sunbeams where the motes float like gold dust and your headdress sits tall above your aquiline nose. I'm trying my best to fit it all in, to listen to your tears, to acknowledge your truth, but I need the dust to be gold in the swirls of the air.

Because you are wrong too in your squalor and your pain. You are crawling, broken in the corridor, the very picture of contagion, of pestilence, of plague. Your hunched lines are not true and strong, your clothing sticks and catches where it should gleam and glide, you do not even weep the priceless tears of the penitent. But despite it all it's true that he loves you. (And this is why my confusion is honest.) If the appearance of selfless dedication to your need, if the gentle taking of your sweating hand, if the daily swell in his throat matched by the nightly swell in his groin is love, then he loves you, really he does. He may be unsure of it, and you may not know. But he loves you, has after a fashion both kissed you and held you, has stayed by your side through the long, long days. But now I know I see it. Finally his patience is paying off. And that's where my hope lies.

For example: today when he visited you walked together in the sun. (It's true, you told me, though still you had no smile on your face, much less in your eyes.) You walked together up and down in the garden. They had made you shower in a wide open cubicle with a fat nurse at the door and antiseptic soap. Now your hair was damp and you shivered like a ghost. (I acknowledge the picture is not yet complete.) But you walked together up and down. Green grass. The flowers, still here after all these days. Warm air playing across your faces as you walked hand in hand through the gardens. Romance.

Do you feel it? You must. What have you noticed now you're out from your room? What do you see in the newness of air, and light, and green?

Look, by the border, a family group, the mother seated on a bench, and the father six feet away with a young child. The child is almost walking. Look! Left hand balancing in the air, and right holding tightly to Dada's finger, it takes a step forward. It pauses, rocking back and forth, held by muscles getting used to doing something new, pulsing with blood fighting newly against gravity. It stands. Then as its father pulls gently forward it sways, stumbles, takes five hasty steps, feet turned in but never quite catching each other, left hand flapping doggy-paddle at the air. Suddenly confident, it holds its balance, then lands headlong, laughing, on its mother's legs. You see it is almost enough to wake her, you watch her hand twitch to crawl from her knee to the soft wriggling back of her youngest child. And then his father, watching, rescues him to run the sequence again, in hope each time of a different outcome.

What else do you see from your place on the path? What do you see in the bright fresh air?

You are walking hand in hand, and when you stumble Peter slows with you, without ever quite allowing you to stop. You are moving, which is good—simply by being outside you are expanding your worldworld. It is no longer darkly square-cornered, but holds the heavens in its dome. Your step strengthens. There are creepers round the windows of the gothic wing bathed in the afternoon sunshine, sheltering birds in their tendrils, holding them safe despite the prospect of night. A blue tit is nodding at the window, his wings chattering as he balances, and flutters, and settles, only to fly round the corner and out of your sight. Peter sees with satisfaction the movement in your eyes, the twist in your neck as you twitch to follow the life that is darting and ducking in the breeze.

Your feet and his crunch in time on the path. You walk to the end, pause, looking out at the hills beyond the town, you turn, you walk back. The blue tit has gone, and the sun has shifted, deserting the creeper, but turning the windows gold.

You are moving closer to taking back your part in your life. From nothing you became clay-like, taking the impression of small realities around you. The weight of your limbs set up an ache in your hip; your knees scraped on the floorboards and your skin reddened in sympathy; you drank and your veins swelled to fullness. The signals have begun to return to your brain. Your responses are logical, have a prompt and a purpose, are connected to facts of life which are shared by the people around you. When they are cold now you are too. You work with your body to save its warmth.

VII

By the next day it is simply a given that you will move on your own beyond your room and into the corridor. It is no longer acceptable that you might stay in bed. You were tired when they woke you to give you your pills, you lifted your head up on your elbow, collapsed again while the sip of water was still in your throat. But despite that, by mid-morning your curtains have been drawn apart and though you smart at the light you feel your muscles flickering to move. There is a nurse too, insistent by your bed. It becomes clear that the things they want now come in twos. 'You need to keep drinking', she says, and you nod. 'Will you have a glass of water now?' You feel a thickness in the back of your throat. 'OK', you say. And now the next challenge: 'Come with me. I'll show you the kitchen.' You look into the distance as the chunks of thought drop into place across your brain. You blink. 'Yes,' you say. You don't move.

'Come on, sit up,' and the voice is surprisingly kind. Tears swell up under your eyes, but what she is asking for is not sadness but movement, and that, it appears, is now something that you know how to do. With her brown hand she takes your pale arm and step by slow step you approach the door. Your hand trails behind you across the wall, catches on the ridged doorframe, grips it briefly before coming loose into the expanse of the corridor. You still rock on your heels with a spasm of pain as you leave the place you know, but now some of your heaviness has gone and you can look up and around. What you see is distance, and perspective, and a link that goes from here to there. Much bigger than anywhere you have ever been, it nonetheless is a space through which you can walk, and so you are led down to the end and into the kitchen on the right.

In the centre of the room she lets you go, steps away to fill the kettle, turns her back. You take two independent steps to the window. You lean on the wall. You look out at the blue and then in at the flowerpots on the windowsill. The nurse leaves the kettle. She comes to look at the flowers with you.

'You like daisies?' she asks, in a singsong-dissonant voice.

'Yes,' you say, and you look at the potted orchids, three of them ranged in living elegance along the gloss-painted sill.

'Beautiful, aren't they?' she says, taking one of them by its long stalk and turning the flower so you both can see. 'I love daisies,' she says.

And you say, 'yes' and you are overcome by a tiredness that runs from your toes to your scalp, and you drop both your hands and all of your weight is taken by the shiny wall. Something in you almost rebels, but maybe (the thoughts are slow to link together in your head) maybe these fleshy leaves and fine-suede flowers are, as this nurse says, daisies and not orchids. And if they are not there is no value in saying so.

The nurse pours hot water and cold milk onto a teabag in a mug, and puts it down next to your hand. You look at her, your head raised on your newly-strong neck, and you start to say 'thank you'. But even as you speak there is shouting in the corridor and your quietness is extinguished:

'No, no! I won't do it and you can't make me. No.'

And, softer, firm, in a male voice: 'Hold her there. That's

right; hold her arm like that.'

'Like that? Just give me a hand,' with Indian-accented hesitation, and behind it there is scuffing and a bang, and then another bang.

'I'll call my lawyer, I want to call my lawyer. I'm not psychotic, I'm fucking not psychotic. You have to let me call my lawyer.'

Still the other voice: 'No, take it like that, now, together, over it goes.'

(And the first voice now is closer to a scream.) 'No! You can't do that. It's not fucking legal for you to do that. I want to call the police. Let me call my lawyer.'

'Oops', the nurse says, and she waddles out and through the doorway you see a woman half-pulled, half-carried past on the floor—no, my dear, no, it is not me—and a high-pitched alarm now is sounding and still the screaming goes on:

'No, you can't do that. You can't. I don't want it. You can't make me take it. You can't fucking make me.' (And then something muffled that you do not hear.) 'No, I won't. Let me call the police.'

And: 'That's right. Hold her still. No, straight in; no, don't protect the clothes; there's not much blood.'

In the background you have sunk down onto the floor. Your neck is weak again, bent over by your again-weighty head. Your knees are by your chest, you are as small as you can make yourself: you are tight, tense, disappearing into your own mind's world.

Nothing happens. You are still. But then at some point the screaming stops and as abruptly the alarm is turned off; and with that your limbs begin to shake.

Later on they will come and take you back to your room. In the meantime the tea sits and cools beside the daisies.

VIII

And:

touchingly pathetic, that last scene, yes, I agree. A sharp juxtaposition of the brutal with the fine. Worthy of its place in our lengthening talc. Yes—well-judged. Delicate but strong. They cannot say that I have lost my touch.

But despite that now we must progress. The scene changes here. I am moving on. And though you are alone and though your tea is cold, you too must put current thoughts to one side. For we are turning to an episode of far greater import. This, I tell you, is it. The moment has come: the point at which we two come together, we meet.

(You're looking somewhat blank, but that is because you do not yet understand. You will come to be more grateful than you seem to be now. You will thank me. You will even be ashamed of how you are. But in the meantime we will continue. You must have faith.)

So. Chapter one. Our Meeting.

You will note, my dear that I have watched you for a while, and then some. I have seen you through the stages they all go through: you have slept like a princess, awoken and sobbed like an imprisoned queen. Your repeated swoon was automatic as you warmed into life. Your face developed like an old-fashioned photograph, blank white coalescing into features and revealing in colour what theoretically had long been imprinted there. And then you moved. You walked and it was miraculous, you struggled, you slept, you cried, you dreamed and you lay, awake, in the early hours of the day. You can tell that I have watched for you for some time. Not only watched, but watched over you.

And now you have come in turn to notice me. Tell me. What do you see?

Let me help: it is afternoon. I am serving tea with deft grace; as though this is what I was born to do. My hair has been done this morning (a lady comes in), and its silver grey, together with the lilac of my silk blouse, is perfect to highlight the violet of my eyes. (Yes, an unusual colour; but that suits me, I think. You will of course decide how unusual I am, but I think you will conclude that this peculiarity I had from birth is apposite for the lady I am.) A proper tea is something I always insist on. Too many people (watch them – there's one right now), too many just put a bag in a mug and gulp it down as they lean against the counter. (Do not say I did not warn you.) But it is proper to lay it out, piece by piece, as I do. Yes, the china's my own; on my husband's side from great aunt Amelia. French. Nineteenth century. I had to smuggle it in, a piece or two at a time when I went home on leave; no-one was using it in that dusty house. And here I serve tea every day. A sandwich, my dear? (They make them for me at night, and though a little dry they're adequate still the next afternoon. Ignore the crusts; that they didn't understand. They're foreign. But the ham is good, don't you think? And I've quartered them; that bit I do myself.) Do take another. The other guests will be along shortly. I will call them and they will come. I'll call out to my twin boys and they'll come.

But not yet. And so in the meantime let us digress. For I wish to propose a pact to you. This is the reason for my approach.

(My dear, do not recoil. Do not be alarmed. Here, sit down. You see there's nothing to fear.)

Here is what I suggest:

That, bound together in this circle of hell, we talk fondly like sisters and we share our stories. That together we unveil what has happened in your life to bring you here, what is happening now, and what the future will be. What, and why, and what it means. That we work to create your tale.

(Your nod is tentative. But the doors are locked and you have nowhere else to go.)

Listen: long ago I was a writer. Novels. Romantic novels. A little different, I agree. But nonetheless I have the skills; I know what to do. And so I will navigate you through the story that you think is yours, what you believe you experienced, and therefore what you need to understand and to tell. Because some day you will be different from how you are now, and you will want to know how different that is. That is reasonable. I understand it. I respect it. I will try to write what you want me to write in the simple words in which you want me to write it. Throughout you will feel me securely by your side.

But this pact is two-sided. If I am your voice, then you also, you must agree to be shaped by me. By and by I shall also trust you with my tale. You, with your blonde beauty and the quicksilver shiver in your hands, you are the frame on which I want to stretch it. I will write your tale, but in my own way.

(You nod again. Still hesitant. Your eyes flicker at the room behind my head.)

I warn you now that this will not be easy, that laying a clear-worded contract out will not neuter all disagreement. At times you will hate me. But it is in the nature of things that my version will be as true as yours. It will sound as though it is something else, but it will be equivalent. And that equivalence will help you. It will help you to find your truth.

Think about it. Pause for a moment. Think carefully, then come back.

I can wait for a while. I can sit here in comfort, allow my eyes to travel around the room. I can count up the pictures, check that the three clocks are all telling the time within an acceptable bound of accuracy. I can note that the walls are newly repainted, but that the gloss on the skirting boards and on the door is chipped. It is chipped, and on the door it is dull where it has been pushed on and handled over many years. I can tell you that my chair is more comfortable than yours. (I have tested them all before. Perhaps by this stage you can already guess that.) See, now your bones are suddenly weightier and you shuffle your limbs in unease. Then you stop. You nod your head. You say 'yes'. You agree to our pact.

You agree to it. And then you tell me that already you have something that you want to say. I am surprised. I thought that I was ahead of you here. You say no. You say you have met me before today. You say that I must write that down. And so I do; I record it. And this I record in turn—I do so only through gritted teeth.

And this is why. You claim—and it is in the imbalance of your mind—, you claim you saw a vision striding barefoot at luncheon across the dining room tables. (You were sitting there, apart; it was your achievement that day.) You claim she was wearing my pearl ring. That claim is an approximation to blasphemy. It was not, cannot have been me. You say her hair was loose, you say that it was flat above her ears and fanned out like hawthorn sprays around her head. You said she swore and, arms-out, stamped her feet from table to chair to table. That the few patients sitting blankly around the room were quiet. That her skirt billowed against the plastic beakers and plates wet and weighted with thick-set gravy. That her face turned red, suffused outward from an initial pin-prick in each sharp-boned cheek. That the supervising nurses turned their attention to her, but that they watched and left her to pick her way loudly, and then more gently, and then with real care, until she stepped from a chair to the floor and collapsed in the corner, and then they took her in their arms, and they led her, sobbing, away.

I cannot believe that you thought this was me—that you could think—that you could dare. Of all the people to pick on here—of the loonies, the freaks, the fucking psychotics (and my voice, I fear, is shrill and over-precise as I shape the unaccustomed words)—of all of those excrescences on the world you claim that this was, that this was—see, I struggle to utter the thought—you claim that it was me.

But, no, no, I recognise that I forget myself; I need not call for a nurse; I need not dismiss you in rage. I have learned how it helps to respond. Look: I can be calm about this, my dear. (And though I hesitate I can spit out the words, 'my dear'.) I can react with equanimity, be strong in myself. Watch me. I can breathe deeply and focus my eyes on your face, can say simply and truthfully that 'your effect on me just now was a little upsetting.' It was something you said (inadvertently, I'm sure) that made me cry. I do that sometimes, yes, when it all gets too much. It's the pills that make me weep. (See, I take your hand; all is forgiven.) They make me swallow them, I tell you, and so sometimes I am a little upset. But no matter. I forgive you. We are confidantes once again. We were saying how it was that you and I met. And I'm sure I must have introduced myself: Iris. Iris Buchanan (Iris Sketchley as was, but that is now a long time ago). My husband's David, the Buchanan family. Down in the country largely, but also a place in town.

They said I added an artistic glister to the Buchanan name. My novels, you see. When we were first married. Yes—do have more tea—it was a bit of a surprise for some. But the family could not have welcomed me more.

We married in May; I was a late-Spring bride. Flowers all down the aisle of the solid little church where the vicar had known him since he was a boy. Sprays of freesias scenting out the place, freesias embroidered too on the whole length of my train. Of course we mingled the guests on his side and mine. Made no sense to hold to that tradition. And some of my family were unable to come. David understood the situation of course. 'Sketchy attendance from the Sketchley side,' he said and they laughed and I joined in with a delicate feminine tinkle, smiling up at his face; because then I believed that he understood.

And of course he loved me. We were in love. So much it didn't matter that after a while he preferred me to keep the house and not to write. We were stereotypical love birds, I tell you, kissing and pecking in the best of plumage in the bright warm light of the end of Spring.

But the tea, the tea is cold, you say. Yes. I'm afraid that is usual. People say they will come and then they are not here. I call out to them but they do not come.

IX

But to you it seems that they do indeed come. Or, to put it more precisely, that lovely boy Peter comes and so you are back in the garden, back in the sun and holding his hand. And I, my dear, I envy you. Let me tell you why: right now you have everything that you had when you walked together before, and you are also gaining something new.

For right now as you walk together across the lawns your heart is beating fast. There are good reasons, several of them: your blood is low in glycogen, your head is hot in the sun, your muscles are weakened by your time of pure stillness. But (and this is really not yet strong) you are also on the brink of self-consciousness: you now know you are walking hand in hand with Peter in the garden. You know it, and you need it to continue. This is not the visceral need to turn over, nor is it the pre-primitive cry of need not to exist. You are beginning to be reconciled to at least the fact of a current existence, and with that you are returning to emotional need.

This is not love, but it is human at the least. Human, and not yet quite wrong. Your heart is reaching out as your mind did before it. But where your mind moved without friction out and back, leaving you undisturbed as you floated on the tide, your heart's pulses are jerky and they snag on contact with the world around them, as though each pulse were composed of a handful of hooks. Jerking outwards they snag now on Peter, on his smile, on his pity, on the fact that he is here. (The bird is in the tendrils, its nest held safe. It is preparing itself for the oncoming night.) You cannot help feeling the warmth of his hand, and it comforts you. Though you do not know why, you turn your face away when you stop together to look at the hills. You are almost self-conscious; he now means something to you.

On one level this is simple: once again you are human, near human at least, and therefore (as they say) you think because you exist and you think of him and feel him because he is here. (It's a helpful proof that this really is progress.) But let us not take this moment lightly. Self-consciousness is dangerous as well as new. For until now you have been nothing. You have seen shadows, and revelation in the hairs on the back of your hand. You have heard a fly. You have seen the sun, and a bird, and the trees. You have merely neighboured reality, have observed it without any sense of response. But now you are falling from the innocence of your rebirth in which your collapsed mind has held you apart. You are falling sharply into an adulthood bristling with expectation, where your need for love and Peter's offering of compassion may be complex, where it may hurt both you and him. You are moving towards a humanity for which you are not equipped. Do not take this moment lightly. Tread gently on the paths. This time too will never come again.

It is because you are now human that you (with your heart) cling and weep as Peter tries to leave. Close still in the knowledge that you are not yet alive, Peter cradles your head, rocking you gently. (You feel his pulse beating beyond what you hear.) This is safe, he knows, as he abandons himself to this moment, where he is not, he believes, conscious of the fact of you except as an object of need—maybe also of hope. He smells again your sweet, damp hair and the antiseptic tang of the soap. He rocks you. There is no-one else. He has made you live, so it is him you need. You are intertwined, and his compassion for you will be everlasting.

X

When Peter leaves you fall instantly asleep, more soothed than you ever have been. You lie unconscious through the rest of the afternoon and through supper-time, and they have to wake you to give you your night-time pills. When dark comes your mind again drifts away.

But then in that dark you are newly responsive to the world. Every hour a nurse pushes open your door and shines a torch across the room and into your eyes, and each time you half-raise your head, try to say 'hi' though your mouth is soft with sleep and produces only an inarticulate bulge of sound. Each time is the same to you, the gentle click of the door, the skimming light, the heaviness of responding, of proving you are here and in control. But over the hours the occurrences stack up and though what you are proving is that you are half-asleep, what you know with increased certainty is that you are present and awake. So when the early morning comes you are unsurprised, are able calmly to lie, eyes closed, holding yourself safely in balance between the night and the emerging day. Lying in the still warmth of your bed, many hours before he could possibly come, all you allow yourself to know is that you are waiting for him. For the first time you feel no dread of the day. Your body is remembering that cradled feeling, that sense that the world is a protecting embrace, that there is a solidity within the heat of the summer day which now in memory seeps into all that you are. You lie, satisfied, and you wait.

Peter's non-appearance is a gradual realisation to you. Through the early morning as you drink your tea, take your pills, shower, dress and breakfast your concentration is on every task in turn. You still need the force of all your shattered mind to switch on the shower, step into it, soap your hands and across your body, to take the towel and rub yourself dry, to pull on yesterday's clothes which are heaped on the floor. When you are dressed you lie on your back on your bed, head propped on the pillows, looking at the ugly Van Gogh poster on the wall. Thoughts ride trackless through your mind. You are strong enough that every hour or so, without being pressed, you walk to the kitchen and make yourself tea in the same limescale-filmed cup over and over again until the caffeine shakes your hands, your stomach churns with emptiness and your mouth tastes of soured milk. (All of that is an achievement for you. Even the soured taste.)

As you make your repeated journeys to the kitchen eventually your face opens and you and I begin to talk again. Our second conversation.

I am sitting there, at the small table, waiting for no-one, knowing that people will come, will pass by. You remember me there? I'm so pleased. (I knew that I was doing you good.) At first we are as though in colliding worlds. I offer you the loan of my teapot, and you look at me as though you do not know what a teapot is. (And it is a fine teapot; French, nineteenth century–perhaps I told you that before?) I suggest a sandwich and your face pales with confusion. Then, next time, 'you are distracted,' I say as your right hand fidgets at the orchid leaves and your eyes look out of the window and away. 'Yes', you reply, and you are quiet and the leaf turns darker and wetter in your fingers until it is the colour of hospital-cooked greens. We both listen as the kettle draws towards its boil. And then from the middle of nowhere you say as though you are taking a momentous step: 'Maybe he will not come.' Then you are silent, still. You stand and you bruise the orchid leaves and your fingers become sticky and you watch the flower heads sway to and fro.

'Don't you just love daisies?' a voice sings out, somewhere behind you.

But I do not hear that voice. 'Maybe he will not come', you said. And that, I know, is it; that is the key. In a flash of genius I understand what we are here together for. 'I know exactly what you mean!' I say. This is my moment! and my face lights up. I am eager:

'I call for them and call for them and yet they do not come,' I say, and may the Lord bid my mind to hold firm at that thought. 'They do not come, they do not come,' and then, prophetic, 'and just the same he no longer will come to you.'

I half-see a twitching response cross your face. I ignore it. We are the same here, my love, and therefore I can help you, can empathise, can tell you all you need to learn.

(Against my will I become excited as I talk, words toppling out of my over-full brain.)

'That is why I am here,' I say. 'Because I call and I call and there is no reply.' My brain turns faster, and as it whirrs its colour darkens to a deep purple-red. 'They tell me that I should give up my waiting, should be quiet, that I should be gentle, peaceful, that I should be good. They are wrong, my love! They set out to deceive me, to make me believe that light cannot come, to make me desert my angelic boys. No! (No!); I depend on them, and I, and we, will wait until they come.' (I feel my mind excited, but I can ignore that. I do ignore that and I continue.) 'That is what the pills are for, they say, to help me expect there will be no reply, to stop me from waiting, to make me give up. But we will not give up. We will not give in. Here we can stand together' (and I have stood grandly up in my sweeping long skirt, and I have crossed the room and I take your hand and it is dry and it is lifeless in mine): 'we can stand together and though there is no reply we will wait here until there is a reply, we will wait for them. No! We will not give in.'

I pause for breath, but still the colour breathing through my skin is eloquent, is radiant. I stand here in glory, here in the little kitchen with your hand in mine. I say again, less certain, 'We will wait though now there is no reply.' Then I breathe in again, and then abruptly I am still.

You are looking at me with surprise. I let your hand go. I am suddenly overwhelmed by tiredness. I step back, and I say, 'I am helping you, my dear, that is all.' I say this because I know a truth which is beyond you now, and that truth is this: 'Why should Peter come?' I ask you (and I ask it reasonably). 'What is there here for a beautiful boy like him?'

'Look at you,' I say, and then I am more certain: 'look: why should he come here except for tea with me?'

And that is the way in which I find how you care. You look at me. You are perplexed; there is a hesitation in your eyes and your lips purse in confusion. Then you light up from the inside. You say you want me to swear on my grave that I said nothing to drive him away. Your face is pale and there's an oily sweat on your nose. You tell me to swear. I do as you say. I swear it to you, of course I do. Then I stop, and I stand, and I watch you as you shudder from your hair to your bare bent toes. Ungratefully you turn your back, and you slide, lizard-like, out of the room and away down the corridor. You close the door of your room behind you.

It is then that the final remnants of your warm certainty dissipate and with them your mind's tetherings fail. You are back in your bed, blocking out with the duvet and pillows everything you can block of light and sound. You are holding their softness tight and hard down against and around your skull. Your breath is hot and damp by your mouth. With all the shaking strength that you have you are willing time to stop, willing your brain to fall into whiteness. Every sound becomes lodged like shrapnel deep inside your mind, until a new pain crystallises which slowly becomes all that you can feel; and with that pain you arrive in a different place. You are motionless apart from your breath. You are knit as tightly to yourself as you can be. That is what you are.

And that is where they find you. They have routinely checked on you several times before one of them comes and sits at your side, removes the pillow from over your head and asks what is wrong. Tears seep from your closed eyes and run across your sideways face. Then it is your awareness of someone else's breathing presence that breaks your control apart.

We could say that your shaking sobs are communication, but if so you do not have the comfort of a response. So let us say instead that you are building an anti-monument of pain, that you are giving in to all that pain can mean to you, all that it can be. Part of your mind at first remains conscious; you know that you are crying, then that your tears are accompanied by sounds which lurch out of your body and are rationed by your gulping breaths. But then you begin to lose that sense. Your body is convulsing with the dull wet heave of mixing cement, repeated, automatic, heavily inhuman. Chemicals are being released and responded to faster than you can register them. You move from control to observation and then to mere presence. Your heavy self writhes against the sheets emitting a rising, screaming tune which you do not care that the world can hear. And then as the pain bursts inside your forehead you find that you know nothing. Your arms flail. You hit out at yourself, at the bed, at the nurse who tries to prevent you from harm. You have bypassed your cortex, bypassed the subtleties of evolved human thought, and are responding only from your reptilian brain. This is more than hysteria, more than a fit. You half-hear the rhythmical screams and shouts, and deep inside you acknowledge a self-indulgence that goes deeper than thought. Right now is the first time you have let go completely your grip of your self. Hard upon its heels, your terror explodes in a physical realisation that you have lost everything you are, that your self has been borne away.

You will later find out that your body can sustain that level of alarm only for twenty minutes or so. But for now all that you come to know is that behind your dervish response there is a voice. It instructs you to put your feet on the floor, to feel weight on your heels and your toes. It tells you to lock onto the sounds around you, onto its own words, the distant sound of the TV, the further sounds of the people outside your window. And slowly, slowly you come back to here and your breathing settles and then your sobs subside. Only then do they give you the sedatives which you place with shaking hands into your mouth and the half-cup of water on which you choke. Within fifteen minutes you are unconscious.

And that, my dear, is how it comes to be me whom Peter sees that day. It was, you will understand from our piecing together of this tale, that way through no secret cunning on my part; it is certainly not my fault that you were deep asleep. I heard you screaming—we all heard you. Your screams echoed down the corridors, cut through the noise of the turned-up television. As always with these events, there were patients who paused curiously by your door, watching your writhing torment as though to distance themselves from their own. I came, of course, to see how you were, but saw I could offer no direct assistance (saw that you were in your own hell and that I could not reach you from mine). And so instead I waited by the door for your lover; yes, I waited to help him though I could not help you.

He arrived at four. Tea time. And we took tea, and I told him that sadly you could not be here. (He talked also briefly to the nurses, but did not, of course, open his heart to them in the way that he did to me.) He came, I say, and we talked, and then he went away.

Now you are looking up at me in hurt surprise. You say how could I not have said this before? You look as though there has been a betrayal. But what could I have said? That he came and we took tea? Why is that something that I should have told you? No, there was nothing to say. No, no, he gave me nothing to give to you. No, certainly not. (And may my voice not betray me here.) Why do you ask? (May that skittishness not let itself be heard.) We simply took tea together, he and I, I tell you, and he stayed for a while but you did not wake up. Your chapter with him had already ended, my dear; that last hour of his company was purely for me. And by the time you awoke he had gone.

You look at me in shock, and your face is white.

XI

For the record we have taken a slight pause here.

You say you need a moment to recover, a time to catch your breath. You look harshly at me as you say that, but I refuse to bear this responsibility. I am, though, prepared to wait for you, to wait until you have rebalanced your mind, remembered what it is that you owe to me, and though for a while I see you struggle to breathe calmly, see your face darken and your shoulders clench up towards your ears, I also see you regain your self-control. You remember that you need me to tell your story. You nod. Grimly. 'Yes', you say. And so, let us set off again:

The pills hold you only for a couple of hours; it is only in the evening that you wake, but even then your jaw is set tighter. That hardness expands as all evening long he does not come. And then you sleep and you wake and over time the hardness develops into a certain confidence. From that afternoon something in you has changed. Something in you that was fragile has been crushed and thrown away. It is as though your screams have shown you the worst, and you have emerged again stronger as a result, but no longer expecting as much from the world. You follow with less difficulty the hospital routine, and they praise your efforts, and the summer wears on, and then suddenly your brain is recharging so fast that his impression is being crowded out.

You now wake automatically in the morning, collect your pills without a reminder, prepare yourself for the day. When the tasks are done is when you and I talk; this is the time of our greatest talks, our heart-to-hearts, our sharing (in this hell, we remind ourselves), our sharing of our two true souls.

For instance, I talk to you about painting. We go on an art tour around the ward, note together the Van Gogh still there on your wall and inspect the blue-framed Monet on mine. The nurses watch. They are pleased that we're engaging calmly with each other (they say so); and one of them produces from the back of a forgotten cupboard some large sheets of creased, rough-grained paper, and a cardboard box of stubby, muddy pastels. 'Why don't you try some drawing yourselves?' they suggest. 'It will be therapeutic. Creativity. Expression. Better than in words'. We are biddable at the moment. We sit between meals at the plastic dining tables and we do as we are told. You measure out with rigid precision a symmetrical tree, draw in branches, twigs and buds with care, and they tell you it is good that you are becoming grounded and appreciating the beauty of the natural world. I also begin with small light strokes, filling a sheet with a delicate flower meadow like embroidery. (They coo.) But then I toss that to one side and start on the next: a wide arc that is the silhouette of the far off hills, and a figure, escaped, pacing to and fro, and above her a bird which is nearly gone. Then, quickly, child-like, a castle and a river and a shepherd with his flock, a ship on the sea, an abstract bright ball. And finally, sitting surrounded by overlapping, smudged sheets, my brain clears and I draw very simply a bridge, a boat passing under it, the limits of the river, two children falling, and then, before you can see, deliberately I scribble it out in a swirl of red and for twenty-four hours after that I cannot bear to talk.

When I next speak I make a request of you: I ask you in return for my Monet to give me your Van Gogh. The Monet, I tell you, is beautiful. The Japanese bridge at

Giverny, arcing over flamboyant turquoises, greens and purples below; of lilies, of water, of irises. It is beautiful, I say. (And yet it throws my brain. It is the water, the bridge, the sheer looking down.) This is the only request that I make of you. Surely you will see fit to agree?

(For the Van Gogh also is meant for me; that is how they were. Turning every which way to see the sun.)

You agree. You do not care, you say. And so we set out to make the swap. Careful, stealthy, when no-one is looking.

Both turn out to be nailed to the wall.

I am quiet for a little while after that. You keep away. You respect my need for peace, sit in a corner of the television room, and read broken-spined romances. You do not have my support and guidance and so you are purely passing time. You have no response to the words which like an autocue pass before your eyes and then are gone. You feel no sense of satisfaction from the narrative shape, from the developing characters, their trials, their resolutions. You do not even notice their names; each is merely a shape of letters which is repeated, takes up a certain space on the page, makes for you the links in the story. (You are doing more than nothing, but barely. There is no sign of progress, no goal, no motivation, no life.)

But then I re-emerge to help. (As a novelist myself, I am horrified at the rubbish you choose to read.) In your service I rouse myself again to my task, bring out again my notepad and sit, wait, hear your dictation.

So we express ourselves; so the days pass.

Then all of a sudden you are ahead of me. The doctor (whose face you for some time have recognised) begins to talk about your discharge, first as a theoretical possibility and then, as you do not shake and scream or retreat into blankness, as a time-bound act. And then the days have been counted down and you are walking through the long corridors for the last time.

We take tea together to say farewell. Just the two of us, together in the kitchen, expecting no-one else. We both know exactly where we are. I have in front of me your story so far, written crabbed in this silk-bound book. It is something of which we can both be proud, I say, and you nod and you sip at your tea and your eyes fill with tears. But I am now strong enough that I can be strong also for you. I say goodbye. I say I hope you go well in the outside world. I say to remember to be as I have taught you here.

You nod.

And though we two say 'goodbye; farewell' all else is as it has been as long as you have been here. The corridors stretch away, and the women in uniforms glide gently along them.

You pick up your bag, push your papers into it, and you turn, and you walk away. You are now without me, my dear; you are alone.

OUTSIDE

I

Your head is down as you reach the hospital doors, hear the click of the electronic lock being released, and step outside. (You do not notice that make-up ravaged receptionist saying a bitter goodbye.) You watch your feet as they cross the pavement and walk down the drive. It is twenty yards to the main road. Ten. Five. You keep your head down, and you shift your heavy bag on your shoulder. Three. Two. One. You stand where the kerbed hospital driveway meets the real pavement. You take a breath for yourself, to prove you are in control, and with that pent tight inside you you look up.

What you see is a series of bright-coloured shapes. They are layered on top of each other, and all of them are shifting. Like a pack of cards being roughly shuffled face-up they are interwoven, unwoven, fading in and fading out. Each colour moves at its own speed and in its own direction. Its shape changes as it moves.

You blink, and again you blink.

(You have been through these gates before, but always accompanied. This time your exit is permanent, and you are on your own.)

You blink, and then your hearing too cracks open: collectively the shufflings bring with them undifferentiated noise. Just that. White noise, turned up, tuned-in to life. It hits your skin-thin eardrums (so long protected) and pours in waves through the bones of your head. One wave, then the next, in time with your pulse. Your thoughts are swept clean.

You are present. You blink again. Your nostrils flare.

You are terrified. You are right to be.

The shapes move and they are nothing you know. Their noise is purely meaninglessness. Both shapes and noise are concentrated by your unpreparedness into a solidity which shocks and overwhelms you. Your eyes fill with tears. You are (let me acknowledge it again) overwhelmed. But slowly as your eyes and ears absorb what is around you it becomes clear that at the very least you can stand here for a few moments and survive. You think that perhaps the shapes are moving towards what is for each of them a goal. And then the next thought finds its way through the noise and into a quieter space in your head: and you know that what surrounds you is a distortion of something that once was familiar and real. You find that you can stand and wait. The coloured shapes move. But you discover that you can break them down. That some move faster than others and you cannot follow. But that some are almost still.

You pause. (This is a triumph.) And then with the greater strength that comes from survival you let out your breath. You force your eyes into focus. You stare.

Let me tell you what you see:

The street is a complete world; bigger, brighter, busier than anything you have ever seen. It is crowded from where you are right to your far horizon. (You flick your focus out as far as it will go, to check, and then you pull it back.) In front you see a man paused side-on to the road. (There is traffic beyond him, and more people beyond that, appearing and disappearing with the changing lights.) He has a buggy filled with carrier bags and two differently-small children beside it. They are a distinct, a composed group. None of the three has registered your arrival.

But you need to continue to survive. And so you have brought your eyes up from your feet, and then from the road, and then back from the distance to focus on these near-static people, and so theirs is the world with which you first begin to re-engage. They form a whole which is held distinct from everything else. You watch them.

The father has one ankle cocked against the buggy wheels to hold it in place, and he is tapping, face screwed to tightness, at his phone. He is oblivious to the road and to your appearance. But he is still talking to his children. (You listen; his words begin to separate into something you understand.) 'Yes, Sam, we're going home to Mum'. And, 'No, not yet; leave Dad alone'. And they pull at his trouser-leg and 'No, Mike, get off; will you just let go will you.' Then 'here', he says, and pulls a bag of sweets out of one of the carrier bags and, eyes still on the blue-lit screen, hands them down. You watch. You see how the boys are redirected, how, scuffling, they focus in on themselves and on the bag. Brought together in close concentration, heads down, they pull the plastic open and they chatter and this calms your pulse, so you continue to watch. You see them pulling to-and-fro over the cellophane, feet crunching on the acorns fallen from a solitary tree whose trunk swells, scarred, out of the pavement's tarmac. Their rhythm is innocent, but then it is not. There is a shout and a cry and sweets tumble to the ground as the twice-held-onto bag sheers apart.

Instantly now the situation is different. Now there is nothing that the father can do; now the sweets are one-side-coated in a sheen of wet dust and crushed acorn, and the dust is mingled with tears, and sticky fingers, and so he says: 'No, just leave them alone. No, take that out of your mouth. You've no idea where they've been. What would your mother say?' But the distraught boys know exactly where they've been. They've been in the wet dust which now smells to them like the tears they've smeared with the backs of their hands across their cheeks and into their hair. They are children and so this emotion comes easily; but it is, nonetheless, strong and it is real.

You observe it.

You are still standing there. Still emotionless, still still. This disaster has not touched you. If they stayed, if they talked to you, then you might start to understand what changed and how and what it means. But despite the tears and the rising shouts the family has disintegrated its neat composition and is now moving on and out of view. The screaming is both everything to them and nothing, as though they have jumped into deep water and now are out and have shaken themselves magically in an instant dry. The man is bundling up the mess in a tissue and the remains of the bag, easing them into the over-filled bin on the corner, wiping his sticky fingers on his denimed-thigh, holding onto the buggy and shouting at the boys. And they are largely following, though their dragging feet digress back and forth behind him on the pavement, and they are sulking and silent, and throwing their bodies from side to side. Then their shape changes as all together they near-collide with a hurrying woman who is irritated that her path is blocked, then offended by the family's automatic side-stepping deference to her age.

They disappear out of view. Your gaze is lost for a moment, and then, with relief, transfers to her.

Freed from the family she arrives at the bus-stop and, breathing heavily, settles herself into the queue. She pulls a bright lipstick out of her pocket and reapplies it. It is messy, but it does not matter, because she is next to a woman who really is old, whose shoulders are hunched as she searches in her bag, looking up and down at her liver-spotted husband. He is nervous. There are often no seats, and though they left home early and are towards the front of the queue (he counts, three, four in front of them), there are many more people waiting than usual, and just at their side is a harem of mini-skirted girls kicking and swarming as they avoid the tedium of simply passing time. They too are on their phones, the wires in their ears catching on the gold hoops all but one of them is wearing. He wonders who they are talking to, feels absurdly certain they are communicating with extra-terrestrial life. But only briefly, because he knows that aliens are passé nowadays, that he is a fool and is merely worried they have not seen the queue, or that they will not acknowledge it, that he will not have the confidence to speak up for his bad-tempered wife and ensure her a place. He remembers he once had confidence. That is long ago, and it is much longer ago than he remembers.

A nurse passes in a hurry, bundling off the tunic of her uniform at the end of her shift so that by the time she ducks into the shop for fags she is just a decent-looking, heavy-thighed girl with pale hair lifted into a ponytail that also lifts her smile. She comes out again, passes a dog sniffing at the pavement, and then a girl genuflecting over the detached chain of her bike.

There is a group of boys in shiny tracksuits. One is kicking a football at the wall in front of what was once the Methodist chapel and is now a half-empty and run-down block of flats. He is close to a regular rhythm of leather on sandstone. Bu-bùn, bu-bùn as the ball scuffs the ground right by the wall and kicks up hard onto it and out in an arc to his waiting foot. He is concentrating on the rhythm, unaware of the traffic behind him which hides the ball's timed perfection from his companions. One is absorbed in a game, his minuscule movements aggressively catapulting pixel-drawn soldiers to safety or into the path of streaming gun-fire. Another jostles, watching, at his shoulder. And though it is only early afternoon and still a good day it is as though the light which creates the game is visible on their faces as a flat brightness which has stolen their souls. Bu-bùn, bu-bùn goes the ball, the gun-fire, and the exhaust of the lorry which has drawn up by the kerb. Behind it all the old man's heart defies his pacemaker with fearful anticipation.

In the midst of all this you are nothing. No-one has noticed you standing. And in watching others you have stopped noticing yourself. Your breathing is pulling and pushing at the hairs in your nostrils like the turn of the tide in the weeds of an estuary. But you are not a river of life, not a microcosm of this fragmented street society. You are much less a symbol of the hopes, fears and weaknesses of the world. You are nothing, and you are alone, and you stand with the soles of your shoes on the tarmac-ed graininess of the pavement.

You never see the girls hold off to the back of the queue, do not know the old man got his two seats with ease as the bus drew up and drew away. You do not see the dogs, cars and workers who pass. You stand and you try to breathe and you wait. And what eventually catches at your consciousness is the beat on the wall of the leather-clad ball. Bu-bùn, bu-bùn, bu-bùn, bu-bùn. You are grasped by its rhythm which is something new to you. The hospital offered you nothing insistent. It held you in its embrace and you sank into it. This sound, however, is calling and you hear it. Right now the traffic is lighter and the ball is shaping the air, sending messages in individual sounds to your ear-drums. For a moment you are linked to the boy who has proved that practice makes perfect. This link is a miracle of human connection. And so it is he who gives you the strength to walk yourself the few yards to the bus-stop and to lean and wait against the graffiti-ed shelter.

II

The journey you need to make is one you have made before. You are returning, as your double-signed and photocopied discharge plan states, to the flat you have lived in for the last six months. They have sent no-one with you because this is a journey you know.

It turns out that they were right: you do know it. When your bus arrives you have the fare ready, though you would not have known the value of the coins in advance. You sit automatically near the front on the left, and the streets unfold without unexpectedness. The vibration under your feet has a lulling familiarity. You are safe in your sweat-smelling nylon seat.

You look outwards at the view, at small grey houses connected and curving in chains along the main road, turning off into side streets, drawn in turn inevitably back, each chain attached to the whole by deeper grey pavements patched with holes. There are dark ragged hedges softening the angles of the walls; but then occasionally they are clean-cut, with purple, white and pink flowers clustered at their roots, bamboo canes at the corners and a bird-table flush with nuts in the exact centre of the lawn. There are also, irregularly, people: here it is housewives whose jewel-coloured saris are stuffed awkwardly under winter wool coats and who move only at a shuffle, a pace which is heightened as a runner passes, weaving, between them. It is a time of day when there are few children who are not being carried, few men who lift up their feet as they walk. It is the lull in the day for doing housework in peace, and the world is gentler for it.

The streets pass. You think you are doing well, that you are concentrating on reality as you have been told to do, seeing the view as it really is.

You are doing OK: your eyes are registering what is there. The houses, gardens, people all help to hold you here; they do help you to relax. But seeing reality is itself only a part, and if you were better attuned to your body you would have noticed also a set of minute chemical changes set in chain by the unlocking of the hospital door. Warmed into life by the sweets in the dust they have now with the movement outside the bus drawn together to feed an alertness in your shoulders, in your neck and jaw, individual muscle fibres shortening one by one until, unobserved, whole muscles have pulled themselves in. You do not notice this. Your mind is focused with deliberation on the view outside. You see a young woman in a blue sari carrying an old-fashioned basket full of oranges gracefully past the dented cars whose wheels sit deep in leaves and fast food litter. You see the colours move. But fed by the tension in your shoulders blood is pooling in your muscles' tightness, hoarding energy in anticipation of something to which if asked you would be able to give no name. As she stops and turns and you see her face, that no-name movement is enough to create an alarm in the back of your mind, a heavier darkness which broods over the stem of your neck. You are still unaware of any danger. But your body is doing the job that it has learned: your system is primed; your muscles are ready to run. (The woman crosses at the zebra crossing, halting the bus and passing across from one side of the windscreen to the other.) You see a tremor in your hands and you still them fiercely. You ignore them as a long-overcome aberration. Your brain locks out the worry you should feel.

You can still see the woman. She is rearranging her basket, rebalancing the spheres and their glowing warmth. The bus begins to move again.

But with the effort of denying your hands their shaking reality, denying them the blood which is beating irregular and hard through your arms, your brain, unguarded, loses its hold. The glass of the window by your face thins and then dissolves. The woman, the cars, the litter, the patches in the pavement merge into one and instantly you are above it all. You see that the town is the wormy flesh of a brain. The traffic and its lights are the electric pulses, the transmitters that absorb and release charge, that create the regulation on which the world depends. (And you too depend on regulation.) You blink. You move your feet on the floor. You feel your weight on them and it. It is real. You are well, going home, there is nothing to fear. You focus your eyes deliberately on the view and through the reasserted glass the town re-forms.

Now, you tell yourself, there are shops. They are lined up in rows like an upmarket play-set. The buildings are made of sandstone, but clad in blocks of plastic colour. Each shop's tailored logo shouts at you, clashes with that of its neighbour, pushes itself forward. There is no transition from one to the next. You watch them nonetheless. You count them. But you know that they do not help you. For the tremor in your hands is awakening again, and then it is extended and as you feel your shoulders begin to shake, your breath, too, pulls tight.

You concentrate on looking outwards. You see the brains which are also the streets, which are never-ending yet whose houses all are labelled with a finite number. You see the neural paths flare with messages, and with them the speed of the bus varies, the gears crash forward and the brakes heave back as though the metal casing is itself responding to more than just the traffic lights, the signs and the cars, as though it is almost blindly searching out its path, faltering with care on its way through the world.

And as the pressure in your shoulders and then your chest grips you tighter, at last you acknowledge what it is you're ignoring. You lean to the window and twist your neck sideways, and you transfer your eyes from the bearably-boxed human-sized buildings and up to the width of the open sky. It is vast. And it is alive. You saw it from the hospital, but from here it is different. There it was blue, was calm, was restricted, was the domed heaven enclosing you and protecting you. But here its proportions are different. (In gaps it goes on beyond the town, on and on to its distant horizon; and from there over the sea and frozen continents and over the sea again.) As you look, clouds cross it, are pursued from right to left as though they are fleeing with varying amounts of fear. Below them the leaves they pull up rise and fall in spirals, snakes charmed by a devilish tune. The smell of afternoon bonfires penetrates the bus, and you, too, are charmed, you are lost.

(You do not even feel your nausea rise.)

But you have no time to panic before the bus slows again, and you look down and you see that you recognise the stop. You are shaking and light-headed. But you can still get off, and in that moment of effort you forget the tyrannical sky. And so you enter your building, climb the flight of stairs, turn your key in the lock and are inside your flat with the door closed behind you and your bag is beside you on the floor.

You are still shaking, still faint and sick. And that makes sense to you, because as you look around your unlived-in flat there is nothing firm for your brain to hold onto. So you do the only thing that requires no effort: you give in. You sit on your bed, you let your head tip forward. And you wait.

The cool night falls.

In the end you lie down on your right hand side. For a few hours your shivers dissolve into sleep.

You are still in that position when the sky begins to lighten. But by this time more has changed. It is September; darker, colder, than it has been till now. The world has moved on while you have been locked away.

You watch the angles of the wall and the ceiling as the growing light new-creates them in velvet, and then in plaster. You are missing the impetus to begin.

And that, I'm afraid, is my cue. You promised you'd ask me when you needed help with your story, but even I can see that's not about to happen. So listen to me now:

It is September, and it's undeniably cooler, but still it brings the freshness of a new season. The season is on a brink, as you are. It's fair enough for me to have been patient until you got home, and I've given you a night to sleep in your own bed. Now, however, we both know you need to get a grip. Your narrative needs routine, interpersonal relationships, healthy activities, a relapse prevention plan. You need, in short, to put in the effort. You must still remember you promised me you would. It was a part of our pact. We agreed that you would do it for me.

Try now. Let us say that the walls of your flat have emerged into the classic greys of a Dutch painting, un-peopled. You need to stand to create the Vermeer. The woman musing, melancholy, stepping heavily-shod across the cold room is an advance on where you are now. Try it. Swing your legs down again, put your weight onto your feet. That's right. Now stand, and look out of the window. Even that is a contact for you with the world.

At first you are standing as you are told. But then you are more than just standing. You are straining to see, compelled again by the scope of the sky. This time it is calm. It is early enough that only a few planes have left their spreading laddered scars. And you are facing east, right into the face of the emerging dawn.

Even you know this day-break is something special. Its first glow sits snug against the hard line of the buildings that form your horizon. It picks them out and they burn. And you know it is nonsense to say there has never been such orange, never such white, such blue. But for a moment that is what you feel, and with it comes the sense that the colours are pouring out of your heart with every beat, that they are suffusing your veins all the way to your feet and fingernails.

Suddenly you are not alone. You hear it first, even through the glass: a creaking, honking cry which fragments into prehistoric conversation. You look up, and there, where later the planes will own the sky, is an arrowhead of migrating geese. They move with supreme confidence across the dawn. Your eyes follow them. They are as cut from black paper, featureless; but their order nonetheless is perfect. They are close enough for you to see the slow flap of their wings as they slice open the sky, for you to watch the leader slipstream back and be instantly and harmoniously replaced. They hold you with them, with the purpose of their journey. You are suddenly content with a purity that is perfect stillness. But then, as you watch, the sun breaks open the dawn with a crescent you cannot bear to look at, and you blink at its suddenness, and your heart jumps, and you wipe your eyes. And when you look again they are gone.

III

But after that the world has changed. Your breath is coming more easily; your head is upright and your shoulders softened; your blood-flow is regular. There is a warmth that fans out from your chest as though your arteries emerge from your heart like the points of a star. And with all of that it seems unquestionably natural to you to go outside, to take in the air which has been touched by the geese whose silhouette you still carry on your retinas. So you pick out your purse from your hospital bag, pull on the heavy musty coat from the back of the door, and go out.

It is still early enough that you are undisturbed. Your neighbours are asleep with their curtains drawn—there is one uncovered window in the block and it is yours—and the only movement outside is the street-cleaning buggy laying down its damp trail, snail-like, glittering, in the dusty angle of the gutter. You cannot see the driver, and he does not acknowledge you. And I am also trying now to let you be: you need to start to become the person who will own the rest of your life.

You are alone and beginning to digest that fact.

So, in the meantime a short digression:

You have reached phase two of your discharge process, and that is worth our notice. The first phase is always one of fear. The world is a place of noise, of light, of a level of stimulation that you are simply not used to. It hits you like a series of gritty waves and pushes you back with a force it takes time to understand and to start fighting against. You learn first not to have your breath knocked out of you, then to lift your head and breathe between waves, and finally to twist your neck like a long-distance swimmer, immersed and paddling constantly but taking smoothly the air that you need. With that you can grow from fear to confidence, to excitement and determination. (I know because I've done it several times myself.) At the moment you are still spitting out the grit. But the geese have shown you the possibility of becoming an expert at motion, in water or in the sky. They were beautiful and so you will learn from them. But you must take care, my darling, take care. While you are afraid and forcibly lifting your head for breath, you are surprisingly invulnerable: you are tensed already against life so nothing can shock or harm you. The grazing pain you feel at everything, the salt water you swallow with every stroke, is a price you gladly pay to protect your deeper self from harm. But when your energies are turned outwards, when you are relaxed, that automatic protective cover is lost. Then it is simple: you get the rhythm of your breath wrong and you drown. Or, to change our metaphor, you have sufficient foot soldiers either for defence or for attack. To live you need to risk the attack, but only when it is time; only you can tell whether it is time.

So while you turn that over in your mind, let me tell you about that first time that I was discharged, how I tried to learn to breast the waves.

My care plan was simple: tall, coiffured, grand in my sweeping skirts, I was going home; home to David and to the Buchanan family house we had lived in since that late Spring nuptial day. It was an occasion. You know how it is. I had been in the hospital for several months, long enough for things to change in me. What they said to David was that I was safe, and that the pills would keep me that way. He nodded at that. He was grave. But it was, I tell you, more than that. Through my enforced stay in that terrible place I had achieved a certain humility. I had focused in on who I was. I had reached the stage of being prepared, entitled. I was ready to draw on the strength of suffered illness and recovery to walk out and take up my life again. Not quite my old life, for parts of that still were a blank no-memoried space in my mind. But my own life nonetheless.

And so I turned my back for the last time on the Monet on my wall. I did so without fear. (It was by now long after you had left. I was long past feeling that fear.) I said farewell in turn to each of the nurses who lined up to say their farewells to me. They gave me a bag with a month's supply of pills. I gave them my teapot to remember me by. Then David, silent in honour of the moment, drove me smoothly away.

I arrived back at the house in the country, put my coat down in the hall, watched as David carried my bag upstairs. His mother and sister were there to greet me formally. They had been there through the long days of my illness, were staying on to help him through this shorter time too. They were staying in honour of him and of me.

That night we ate dinner which they had cooked in my kitchen; a meaty terrine served up with salad, and casserole with potatoes dauphinoises. The terrine was layered and pressed to preserve some treasure within, the casserole rich and thick with sauce, the potatoes thin-sliced yet heavy with cream and cheese. (They cooked acceptably well.) We ate. We passed smoothly from course to course. They sipped gently at the wine. They made the conversation. I sat. I ate. I heard.

And all was well. It is true that initially I was a little dazed. I couldn't do David my full duties as his wife. I was, that is to say, spaced out from the pills. (I could not quite remember who I had been before.) But there was nothing for me to do. I had returned not just to him. They too had become for now a part of the household. Their belongings were spread around: dark coats in the hall, new-cut sets of keys in my fruit bowl, insufferably-scented flowers matching the walls in every room. And some of my things had been moved away. To clear space, they said, as on one of my better days I looked, surprised, at the serried rows of heavy boots in the cloakroom which smelt now, incongruously, of lavender, pale blue in the air against the dark leather colonnade at knee-height round the walls.

But none of that was a problem. For in the early days my needs and interests were restricted. I was content to spend the mornings in bed. My mind wandered as the light strengthened and moved around the walls. Then later in the day I walked from room to room, touched the familiar props of my life, smelled without question the fresh paint in a brace of empty first floor rooms. (I never once thought to read or to write. My book—our book—lay untouched by my bed.) I behaved well. I ate as directed. I daresay I was pale and maybe dishevelled (I have seen that in others at about this stage), but really I do not know; and no-one told me.

For they in turn were content for me to move as a ghost among them. They always needed, eyes cast down, to leave when I entered the room, and I moved slowly round, a hand on the furniture, or sat for a while. Occasionally I cried. I was part of a permanent solemnity they felt in the air.

(I know now in part what that solemnity was. I know it now, but I did not know it then. My brain and the pills kept it from me even as those around me also kept away. They treated me as though I was a child or a brain-damaged invalid: an idiot, a fool, a damned soul, one apart. They told me nothing. No-one tried to help. No-one, I tell you, stroked my hand. No-one. Can you believe this? I tell you this—hear me!—I tell you it, and you hear my voice break with sobs: I tell you it on my oath.)

February and March passed in this way. Then towards Easter they left, and something was worse from that point on. David and I were not revived by privacy. I was brighter now. (We were reducing the pills.) I was able to cook, to wash up, to do the laundry, to iron the shirts. I was ready to hold conversations, was prepared occasionally to accompany him out, to lift the net that was over my life. I was ready (and it mocks me to say it now) to be kissed, and held, and whispered to. For him to say that he loved me, for us to walk together through the fields.

I barely saw him. He had moved on my return into one of the spare rooms (to help me sleep, he said; and that was the only way I knew that he acknowledged my nerves were bad). From there he brought me tea in bed every morning, just as his mother had done while she was here. Every morning the knock on the door was followed by his frowning face, eyes focused on the tea cup as he crossed the room. After a while I stopped saying 'Good Morning. Thank you,' but still he appeared and still with the tea, and still he left me as he went to work for the rest of the day. I would rather not have had the tea, would rather he'd stayed in our room for me to waken in his warmth. Even if I'd woken to it throughout the night. Rather my face could have nested in the soft cup between his shoulder-blades. I would rather, I would rather. But what I would rather have had was not spoken.

What weighed on me increasingly as the pills were reduced and as in response my nerves seemed to clear was that I could not remember what it was I had ever done before. I awoke as I had always done to each new morning, but nothing fired my brain with tasks to be done. No-one asked anything of me but to drink my tea. There seemed never to have been something which had been expected of me and which I had failed to do. All I felt was the quietness.

And maybe that was the problem. For time passed. I gave in to the apparent normality of that quietness. I stopped asking questions, even of myself. (There seemed something inside me I did not want to know.) I slept through the mornings. I folded gently inwards again. At most, in the afternoon I sat straight-backed at my dressing-table looking out and down the avenue of trees. I was at one with the garden statuary. And what slowly, thoughtfully, carefully I did as I sat in silent state was to try in turn the perfumes that David had given me. (With each came a remembered stubbled evening kiss, and then his hasty intimacy in the dark.)

I was cautious at first. I was gentle. I tested each one by one, smelling it in droplets on the air, then on my skin, and then again when my pulse had warmed it to roundness. Each one took for its moment all of my concentration. Time shaped itself to my steady progression through the lined-up art deco bottles. (There was nothing else for Time to do.) And through them I learned from my nostrils that I was still alive. If he noticed in the air my testing of the signs of his one-time love then he never said so to me. But nonetheless this game had a serious core. (Let me tell you this, my dear. Listen to me. Listen hard. I offer, I suppose, a warning.)

It was a hot afternoon and I was in my room. Alone, unvisited, unnoticed. I sat and I saw the calm of the trees and through the open sash windows I heard the rustling of the leaves. And my mind opened up to our earliest days. (I encouraged it.) When we were first married. When we were deep in love.

I could smell that love.

I had chosen for that day just a single scent; one of freesias and fresh lime. I had sprayed it onto my wrists, rubbed them together, sprayed it too into the cup of my collar-bone where it created a sheen which slowly, as I watched it in the dressing-table mirror, became again the dullness of mere warm skin. I allowed my mind to wander as it dried. I experimented. I thought that perhaps I was in love—and I smiled—, and beloved—and I smiled more and my cheeks swelled and my eyes were bright. I followed the idea that today I might go downstairs, might run out and down the living avenue (and perhaps my David—and though still I smiled there was a sharp pain in my chest—, perhaps he would be waiting at its end). It was mere whim, you will tell me, as I swallowed down that pain. Mere whim, I told myself. But all the same I thought that I would dress at least, and then perhaps... and I did not say where perhaps (perhaps!) could go.

I crossed the room to my heavy wardrobe. It pleased me after weeks in my dressing-gown to leaf through the cedar-wood hangers like a lady preparing for a ball, to feel the cottons, leathers, wools, silks at different temperatures on my fingertips. They smelled of mothballs and dry-cleaning chemicals. Their colours brought with them parties, dinners, 'occasions'. Dresses hung neatly side by side, but the one on which my fingers stopped was one which had been untidily thrust in, was bunched, half off its hanger. It was a forget-me-not blue cotton frock with a belt and a full, creased skirt, and below it, loose among the boxes, were pale sling-back kitten heels. The combination had a distant familiarity. (Maybe it was the scent.)

Sitting on the bed I took off my dressing-gown and I put the outfit on. Then I sat there, feeling newly lightweight. Girlish, my weight leaning back onto the palms of my hands, I stretched my legs in front of me, pointed my toes inside the shoes. My smile became a spontaneous laugh. My shins were thin-spread with individually-dark hairs, and hairs, too—I could see if I peered—, grew across my feet and toes. But there was no-one here but me to see. (My movement as I turned to check the door released the perfume to rise warm on the air.)

I jumped up and crossed the room, feeling for my balance in the unaccustomed heels. Then again, lighter on my feet, over to the window and back again. Then a third time to the window, with a skip in my step and a champagne effervescence through my limbs. As I turned I threw out my arms in joy, and caught the moment of movement in the mirror, and I paused and I looked.

It was the light, perhaps, and the shadows it created behind me. Or the illusion of youth which I did not expect. The settling of my dress from that joyous pirouette (like the settling ripples in the blue). The scent that awakened a memory. Or just the lipstick smeared blood-red across my screaming mouth.

They say that he found me there unconscious. That there was an isosceles stain of perfume down the pale wall. That I had thrown bottle after bottle to hit the same spot. (The paper was cream and lemon stripes, with curtains in coral velvet, swagged heavily back.) At the foot of the stain the carpet was seeded with glass. My hands were bloody. I had, they inferred, gathered up the chunks of heavy-carved glass. I had drunk the bottles that would not break.

They said of course that it was deliberate self-harm.

That I was a danger to him and to myself. It was all a little thing, I said to them. I just wore a different dress. It was perhaps a little too young for me, but it was only a different dress. They looked at me as though it was too much effort to explain. 'And maybe,' I admitted, and I remembered my mother-in-law's strictures, 'maybe too much scent.' David looked, embarrassed, at the floor. He wouldn't look into my eyes, wouldn't kiss me, wouldn't explain.

And so, my dear, that was it. There, in more than one way, I had to stop. I was back on that horrible ward again. I was punished for something that I hadn't done. I was back among those people without knowing why. (They clawed and they pawed at my mind.) You see perhaps that there are tears in my eyes. That my vision is focused on something beyond this room. I am silent for a moment. Detached, not at peace. This is, I say, my life after all. But no. Watch me. With effort I can draw my lips into a smile. Memories of discharge, I say to you. About learning how to breast the waves.

And I stop again, and again I am silent.

Then I shake my head. But that was then, I say to you, enough, enough. We should remember what our task is here and now. I sit up straighter and my voice again is clear. Let us remember, I say, that I hold the pen for you. For you and not for myself.

We were talking about you, I say, about your freedom, about the determination and excitement which you have found in yourself. Let us turn back again and follow your path. (Let us forget that I am forever damned).

So:

I left you walking through the quiet early morning, giving no sense of the thought in your head, and, I have to say, I'm struggling for an image. The Vermeer was all very good to get you off your bed, but it's served its purpose now you're out in the street. It's too early in the day for Lowry, both too early and too English for Renoir. None of the Italian Renaissance masters will do (nothing—not even the hedges—is geometric enough here). Turner (in oils) could have captured the dawn, but now that moment is passed and none of them is able to show you as, your belt pulled tight around your waist, you begin to move more fluidly along the pavements and across the roads. That foam of blonde hair, tied back at the nape of your neck, the plain, wide cotton skirt nipped out by your coat so a single fold of it flops side to side with your steps, the flimsy, filmy top inside the rough grey of your coat. And then you reach up and pull your hair outwards and down, and twist it up so it is like a bun, and I have it: you, my girl, are a living Degas. The world is still a blur around you, but you have taken form.

(I breathe deeply at that success. The darkness is fearfully close to my heart.)

It will not help you to know you are a Degas, in figure, in movement, in outlook, in form. It does, however, help to explain what happens next:

Your walk may have lacked a harmonious shape, but by the end of it you have bought the food you need. You have also spent purposeful time in the first of the charity shops to open its doors; you have come out with a jumper, a cord skirt and a blouse. They go together. From another you have found a pair of flat boots, chestnut to the lighter brown of the skirt. Your determination is increased by the acquisition of clearly autumnal clothes; they help you tell yourself you have an awareness of time, that there is a future before you in which at least this season will pass.

Who knows if without that determination you would

have made your final purchase. Unlike the others it is not strictly, not at all, necessary, and unlike them, too, it is beautiful. A scarf the green of a mating mallard's most prized feathers, heavy, soft, large enough for you to wrap around your body. You are drawn to its iridescent depth of colour. It is an item which will take you as deep into life as you can currently go; you can imagine wearing it as, true as you can be, you watch the dawn.

IV

Eventually, of course, you move on from sitting curled in your chair just watching the dawn. It is never again so orange or so blue as on that first day. It is often blurred by drizzle and comes perceptibly later each day, so increasingly it is tainted with people and noise. The geese have long-since migrated. But by default it remains the way you ground yourself in each day. And then one morning you sleep right through it.

When you awake, perplexed, the sky is still dark. It is drawn down your window in inky streaks. That is what you see. (By this time it is late October.) But the light has become so much part of your life that you want also to feel what it is that negates it, to be sure of it, to be wet by the rain, to touch its reality. That need to shiver at the touch of the inhuman is how you come to be walking, wispy-haired, through the block of flats at a time when your neighbours are also moving around. For one of them it is a miracle.

(Stick with me here; hang on in. I know that I have had my faults, know I need to let you tell your tale in as plain a way as you can. But this is a point at which the narrative will change, and together we must take note of that. I had my chance to find my prince; this is your chance to find yours.)

You are nearing the front door. Your prince-to-be has rushed in, ungainly, out of the rain and is shaking his micro-umbrella dry, trying to keep the water away from the bags he has over one arm. He is irrationally embarrassed to be caught in this act, and so carries on the shaking longer than needed, and finishes it with what he thinks is a flourish designed to furnish his glance with what he wants to be confidence. You have seen him before: he is the man from downstairs.

He has also seen you, your ankles disappearing up the stairs, your knees coming down, pulling your body unwillingly with them. But he has not seen you before in this scarf in which you are beautiful, and not with the energy in your face which comes from wanting to feel the heaviness of the rain. Looking back he will tell you you were radiant. What you are feeling at his appearance is a growing heat in your cheeks from the hard pain you are swallowing down, which only the rain can help you dissolve.

Despite your pain, however, it is inevitable once he's commented on the rain that the two of you exchange names. You, asked and with nowhere to go, Rachel. He (unasked) is Adam, from flat two, the one down the hall that looks out over the back. Courtyard. Patio. Beautiful for sitting out in the evening. Next summer. Too cold now. Too bloody wet today.

He thinks his skewed laugh is a self-deprecating chuckle, and hesitates as you neither laugh with him nor say what is in your mind, that he is a dripping Gollum between you and the door.

Briefly neither of you moves. Been here long? he asks to fill the space. He is uninterested in the answer; he knows you've been here a while, hasn't noticed it's a good portion of that while since he last saw you. Hasn't noticed how little he's noticed you before. But the question makes you start, realise where you are, how far you have come from where you have been. A while, you say, not that long.

(You are adrift in the day; this is not how you are used to it starting. That means you have no foundation on which to build your statements, no protection against these incursions to your quiet life and soul.)

A pause.

Less convenient living here at this time of year, he says, and adds, not like the summer when you can take the direct route to town through the parks. A mud-bath it'll be today, a mud-bath full of snappy, muddy dogs. (That is all something he is sure of.)

You do not know what to say, so you say nothing. And it is slowly dawning on him that it's a while since he's seen you, that his mind pictures you only in boots and a thick coat, as though you never wear summer clothes. He makes nothing of it.

A longer walk to the shops at the moment, he says, and he gestures at his bags. My God, he thinks, I'm talking to her about plastic bags, and simultaneously a picture arrives in his mind of your scarf plucked from the surface of a lake at dawn to be wrapped, still liquid, around your thin throat.

Nice scarf, he says.

You say, thank you, and you picture yourself hidden entirely by it, reduced to a single, misshapen feather on a mallard's back, disappearing into a camouflaged void.

Another pause.

Well, he says. Well, must be getting these into the fridge. Wet out there it is.

He wriggles a hand out of the bags to say goodbye, and you, already inexplicably much closer to him than you had intended to be to anyone, naturally take it, feel it is rain-damp but hot, let it go. He moves first, down the hall and in through the door of flat two. He does not look back. Then you move.

You have been held back by his conversation, and by the time you are freed the sky is brightening. You go out. There is nothing special left in the day.

It is, however, bloody wet.

V

After that you find you are frequently in the corridor at the same time as your neighbour. He does not claim it is coincidence, but he always manages to look surprised. And you are becoming used to his presence; he is becoming part of your rhythm now the dawn comes long after you wake.

But even so, he asked you out several times before you said yes. You did not actively want to go, but you had run out of ways to say no, and it did not matter, because you felt neither very strongly. When you'd said no it had clearly disrupted him; he had flushed, and you were ashamed. Someone might have seen, and above all what you wanted was not to be seen. But now there is a blinding shock in his eyes as you say yes as well. (You say it was 'OK', not 'yes'. OK, I hear you; maybe it's important. Either way let us be precise. It may help us both to understand.) 'No' was a disruption, but 'OK' is a disruption, too. Either way he colours, blinks and turns away.

You are left waiting to go tomorrow to a pub for dinner and a drink. That makes sense to me. That sounds good. (It could even be said that this is just what you need.) You readied yourself? Let me guess: you thought hard that night about what to wear. You've said no several times (you don't know how many? No matter; he will know when you joke together about it later) so of course you won't dress up too far, and it is a casual pub dinner, so your corduroy skirt and a smart top. A smidgeon only of makeup, and hair tied up and back. You thought of a few lies for what you had done last summer.

You say 'no'. Your flat eyes do not blink. (This tells me

that you truly do not care.) But you knew you were making a significant step out? No, you say again. You saw only disruption in his flushed blinking, and at the extremity of your consciousness there was a flicker of fear, but you allowed yourself to think nothing of it. You say you were left only waiting for the time till tomorrow to pass.

My dear, I pity you on this, your first ever date. You are afraid not with the indulgent butterflies of pubescent longing, but just because fear is what you are. You are nodding. A shiver has twitched across your face. Yes, my dear, I pity you. But my pity should not be your aim. Our end-point is your story. So tell me what you remember. (See: a shadow has again crossed your face; the memory is leaking still, radioactive, from your bones.)

You say you don't know. Firmly you close your mouth.

(I'm surprised. This deliberate reticence is something new to us. You are, I suggest, remembering excitement. Or boredom perhaps. Or a pleasurable guilt.)

Try again, I tell you. It is healing to speak of it.

You pause. Then you open your lips. You pause again. Then you say you remember nothing of that evening, either where it was, or what you or he said. You pause again, and a shudder lifts the weight of your body. (I am waiting. I can be patient. I'd say that where we are now is worth our while.)

You remember, I say. Tell me what you remember.

You push down your body's reaction. You look at me. You know you must tell me the truth. You say you thought it was a coffee shop you went to and not a pub, but then the timing would be wrong, since you know it was evening. That there was a time at the cinema once, but you think this was not it. All you recall is that it was evening, and of course you walked together home.

Tell me why this is what you remember. Trust me, my dear. You can say what you feel. I think that we've reached to the nub of it here, to a pivot point in your tale.

You remember because you saw his excitement. You, cold, were looking from the outside, and so you, so cold, could feel his bright heat. (You shrank from it, perhaps, in fear of your ice? Forgive me. I am flippant, but this is after all nothing but a date. I am trying, simply, to lighten your tone.) Through dinner you had watched him talking fast, a joke, the next joke, lined up like skittles, barely an opening for you to provide a laugh. You remember you sipped the unaccustomed drinks he ordered, and while you sipped he drank. (Endearing, isn't it, the nervousness of the young, the swelling to bloom of a fresh-budded love, the fear of early frost that could yet wither all. I like him, this man, I like his eagerness, his persistence, his nervous gulps of gin, and then of wine. He is bringing you love, and I bless him for it.) You remember that he split the bill. You remember the indignity of his rush to suggest it, his uncouth unawareness that weak as you were you would anyhow have insisted. Strange that that sticks with you, your dignity a double-ended thorn, both deep within you and the first thing to emerge to protect your soft pith.

I am proud of you. You remember more than you thought.

You remember he insisted on walking you upstairs and right to the door of your flat.

So tell me. Tell me why.

You hesitate.

And I agree; let's wait a moment. Just pause, and perhaps I can describe to you what I see. Let me tell you, for example, the look of your eyes. Listen. This, if nothing else, is true.

They are not towards me but the corner of the room. That in itself is no problem. I look more closely. And then, my dear, I am afraid. Your blue eyes' focus is beyond mere middle distance. Their focus, I could say, is beyond focus itself; if Egyptian mummies could preserve their eyes, this, unwrapped, is how they would be. They are superlatively blank. They are invisible shutters locked hard against your soul.

(This is true. Before I had not paused to see it.)

Now I see that your hands, too, are locked as your eyes are locked. Tendons stand out against their shaking cramp, against the rigidity which turns them white in failure to hold your knees in position. And your knees in turn, their power levered brutally through tight-crossed calves, only nearly solidify the dreadful shake in your feet. Your heels skitter in spasms on the floor. (I can make myself sit here relaxed, attempting to relax you. Looking up and down and around the room. But for all my vaunted relaxation your eyes leave me afraid.)

Tell me why you remember he insisted.

You remember his insistence because it may absolve you of ownership and of blame.

The two of you had walked through the dark streets towards home. Your steps were out of time. You walked so that there was a distance between you. Maybe as you walked he told himself a story, that night as the threshold to the rest of his life. Let us speculate that he thought that the signs were good. Certainly he continued to play his part. Every time you crossed a road he stepped out in front of you, moved awkwardly across and round your other side, a macabre chivalry to protect you from the wet gutters. He clearly enjoyed his role as protector, enjoyed fulfilling the societal mandate. You imagine he talked about you, about dinner, about where to go next time. You imagine that you did not talk at all.

And?

The rest comes in snatches, snatched again even now as you dare for the space of individual breaths to release the lock on your jaw.

You remember standing face to face by your flat door. You felt you should move to acknowledge your goodbye. You reached out to offer him a friendly hug.

Now you can see why he thought what he thought. Does that lessen the shock of your twisted head, your thrown-back neck, your shoulders pinned by his arms?

The night before you had said not 'yes' but 'OK'. Does that matter?

What you remember washes over you now in a shapeless darkness.

You remember that you were barely drunk at all.

Then you pause. You shake your head as though it is with madness that you say it, but this is what your senses recreate: a muscled blackness edged with deep-set octopus rings. Dripping, sucking, flaring ridges in curving rows that grip and thrash at your mouth. An action which is darker and older than anything you have known. Still now you remember, and the image is not new-created to tell me your tale, not generated later to explain and magnify your shame. I hear you, I hear and I record it straight: it was born in your mind at exactly that moment; and as now you remember it, as you say it to my face, you are at the same time behind your closed door, slumped, sobbing. You think you remember you were violently sick. The shudder through your body has, I tell you, the strength of orgasm. But even that does not shake your bruising nails from deep in the flesh of your palms. You are more than naked here and now in this dingy hall. And you are bathed in tears. They lie on your face like the lesions of smallpox.

I would pass you a tissue to shroud your violation, but I, too, I am too tense to move.

VI

But though we were both shocked by your telling of your tale—it was vivid, my darling, I agree—, there's a case for taking a different view. I admit that just now I lost my concentration, that I let myself get caught up in how you felt. And you (you cannot deny it, my dear), your perceptions back then were not entirely of the best. Let me put it as clearly as I can: he took you for dinner—don't flap; *OK*, he half-took you for dinner—, and then he kissed you outside your door. That is all. It happens every day. It was merely something new for you.

Tears are still running down your face. But shush, I say to you, shush. I know that the first time is special. I know it. (You look up.) I remember too when it was new for me. No, I do, I really do; don't look so surprised; there have not been many men. Let me tell you while you recompose yourself.

As always I start by setting the scene:

I was eighteen, and back then we were a good deal younger than that would be today. I was on a sort of holiday, staying with mother's sister Ann beside the sea. She had a B&B a few minutes' walk from the prom. A boarding house was what we called it. I served on the tables in the morning and then the day was my own. I was young, I was hopelessly romantic—see, I admit that openly—but still I had no thought of romance being fulfilled for me. (We are not so different, you and I.) Every day that the sun shone warmly I sat on an old towel on the sand with novels I had bought out of my Saturday job wages. I tied a scarf round my head and rolled up my sleeves. I was making-believe I was in St Tropez.

He approached me one day as I sat there on the beach, and he was beautiful. (I tell you at a distance but my memory is true.) He was taller than me, proportioned so that when later we stood looking together out at the sea my shoulders sat neatly under his arm. His skin was pale almost to blueness, close-pored, soft, barely a shadow at five o'clock. His hair was fine and black, and his eyebrows were picked out so delicately it pained me to see them. His forearms were slim. His hands were strong. I had seen pictures of Michelangelo's David and this to me was what he seemed to be.

He introduced himself, asked whether he could take a lovely lady for a walk. I imagine that I giggled and blushed, but his arrival was after all what I was tuned to expect, and so we walked, and later in the sticky-floored bar to which he took me he smiled at my shy request for lemonade. He drank whisky, he said, and that meant I had to drink pink gin. But he was a gentleman for all that through the afternoon and into the evening he toyed with my hands and with what I said. And as he walked me home he kissed me. He told me I tasted of the pink. I tasted, he said, of gin and of candyfloss. Candyfloss, I thought, too, was what his kisses were to me: feathery, soft, incomparably sweet, but then dissolving each into a wet strength. Each time he left me my shoulders shook with life. Each night I lay in bed tracing the delicate shape of my mouth with my newly-sensitive tongue.

The bliss of young love, I say to you. But, sad to say, it was not to last.

For one day I came to meet him as usual in the bar and he was not there. I sat, alone, leaning my fair head on the dark wood panels. I was a little surprised, but not shaken. I was used by this time to the bar. I waited. I had a drink. I drank it half-conscious of the noises around me; they were beautiful as only noises in our place could be. There was a group of young gentlemen in the back corner, their voices rising as the time passed on. I listened to them. I had another drink. I shook my head. I remembered those feathery kisses. I told the barman that my love was beautiful, that he looked—did I tell you?—like Michelangelo's David. He nodded, said yes, poured me another drink, said today he'd already been and gone. I said, 'Oh'. I was trying to be grown-up. I leaned over the bar, whispered confidentially in the barman's ear that my love, my love, though beautiful, was the type of man who would never stay and be real. He looked at me and then he nodded. Said he'd not wanted to say, but there had been other girls. I thought about that for a moment. (I ran my tongue round my lips and remembered those kisses.) But I was young, and I was brave; I decided desertion was romantic and dashing. I had another pink gin.

And so I was sitting cheerful enough but alone at the bar and somebody asked me to dance. He was older than me. He had a hot, red face above his tweed jacket. He was from the group in the corner. He said I looked like a dance would do me good, told me I looked like some sort of tragic queen. And then he introduced himself: David. That made me laugh. And because of that laugh, and though by this stage to my shame I could hardly stand, we danced. Then we too walked together. And when, months later, he proposed, when he gave me a family ring, he chose the one which was a pearl surrounded by diamonds; an acknowledgement, he said laughing, of my tragic grief, but also a hope for joy.

That is how it was for me, my dear. How I met and was carried off by my prince. There was joy for me in the depths of despair.

Listen: the same can come for you.

VII

The next day you are roused to movement by a knock at your door. It is morning, has been morning for some time; you have been lying, dressed, on your bed, not thinking about what happened last night. 'It is me, Adam,' his voice comes through the door. And you cross the room, and you half-open it. And he is there.

He says, 'Hi, there. How are you?'

You nod. You say, 'hi'. You have slept and have awoken. You have pushed away your revulsion. You have told yourself that that is clearly what the world is like. You are reassured that you feel no emotion at his appearance or his name.

He is clearly pleased with how last night went. He says so. He says he was so glad that you made that first move. He'd had no intention of kissing you, had felt it was too early, did not want to shock or hurt you. But then you'd moved into his arms. He had been so glad, and even now as he speaks his blink stops and his cheeks bulge into a shiny smile, a full-face smile with an automatic blush.

(You are looking at him. You are distracted. You are thinking that even in your own flat you are trapped by his physical proximity. It pains you that your floor is also his ceiling, that whatever you say to him now he will continue to hear you as you move throughout the day. Then you realise that you have the dawn and he the afternoon sun and so you are off-set. That is reassuring.)

He is talking again. Kissing you was of course what he'd wanted to do. He says that and he blushes, but as you do not turn away, as you stand there at your half-open door and you seem to smile he does it again in remembrance. His arms are tight round your angular shoulders, his height compressing backwards the vertebrae in your neck. He clearly does not mind that your tongue stays, loose, in your mouth, that it gets weakly in the way of his tongue as solidly it pushes against your teeth. You still gulp for breath, but now you do not reel. (You even link your arms round his waist. You think that is the right thing to do.)

And when finally he pulls his saliva-threaded mouth away and suggests going out together for coffee you take a breath with relief and say again, OK, and you pull on your coat and you go. And with that begins a pattern. For all of that week he is knocking at your door and you mostly answer. You drink coffee with him, and tea. You admit that you have never had a boyfriend, and you keep your face still as he looks into your eyes and strokes your hand and he tells you that he is so pleased, so honoured he will be your first one. He invites you downstairs and you refuse. But he is building his castle in the air. And you, in your fashion, are building yours. For as stiltedly you sit and you talk you realise you are remaining separate. And so you bury your memory of the vulnerability that comes from being forced to respond to another body in proximity to your own. You begin to feel safer in his presence. Your exterior even begins to smile.

(There is something which should alarm you here. You are denying yourself an instinctive reaction to activity in your body and mind. You are cutting your emotional reaction off from what it is that your skin feels. You no longer notice sensations on your skin. As a result you are less human than you were. Less human and also less safe.)

When the following Sunday afternoon he invites you downstairs for tea, you finally give in.

'Yes,' you say to him and you follow him down.

Then you go to bed together.

You say you feel no attraction to this man; that you consciously are holding yourself back from disgust. You tell me that I must write that clearly down. So:

Your soon-to-be-lover is greasily bald. His scalp is mopped by his dark collar, threadbare white at the edges, matching his cuffs. His arm-pits are creased, as are the greyish sheets on which you both are currently sitting while the tea brews on the side (it is a studio flat and the bed is the only place to sit). You are stiffening your nostrils against the thought that the sheets smell. (He is worried by the sheen of several magazines not quite enough hidden by the box of tissues on the floor.)

Dead-centre in the ceiling the bulb is dim in its navy cardboard shade. He hopes it is a soft, a romantic dullness. It is not. The ugly lit spirals are coated in dust; but they are bright enough still to reveal dark piles of clothes in the corner of the room, books which have slid off each other and are heaped next to over-full bookshelves, wardrobe doors hanging open with largely-empty shelves behind them. The book covers are the only colour not navy and grey; you tell yourself their oranges and greens lend a sophisticated glow.

You are not comfortable here, but aside from your flat this is the only private room you have been in for some time. You have forgotten that other people do not live as you do, with your surfaces clear and no belongings visible to show the world who you are. And therefore despite the grime you are intrigued. You take the time to look around, content at least to be where you are. You are still peering into the corners as he twists his head down and kisses you, and as you accept his tongue now unquestioningly you close your eyes against the electric bulb. It reddens your eyelids, first one side of his head, then the other.

You are, as we said, on the borderline of disgust. But for all your disgust you are curious. So curious that after a moment you pull back your mouth, and, still within breathing distance of his face, you say quietly, a little embarrassed, shaping the words carefully one by one, 'I think I might stay here tonight if I may.'

For you this means exactly what it says. (You are not surprised at yourself.) You recognise that staying would be a step, but your recognition is restricted; it is wholly irrelevant to you where that one step might lead. You have, we repeat, detached your mind from your emotions and from your skin; you are stalwartly cold as you face the world. That is how your curiosity about a night here has been born. His reaction, unsurprisingly, does not mirror yours: he (humour me here) does not see you staying the night as a simple stand-alone step but as a staircase, one with heavy, hand-carved mahogany banisters which leads up through a magnificent hall to a room curtained to the floor in draped red velvet. And he sees there the cliché, the glow of the romantically-mutual sex he has not had for a long time. That is the hope you have given him. And so he is now holding his breath.

You do not notice. Your mind is back-lit by an amalgam of films. It is a shame you have never frequented art house cinemas; if you had, your view might be different. Instead your expectations are censored by multiplex economics. You see a man's slow caressing movement and a woman's face straining past some tense barrier and into deep serenity on the other side. You are suddenly warmer than you were. You feel interested, but as though you are in complete control.

You consider it safe to try the next phase. You sit back. You look at him. You say with determination: 'May I lie down next to you?'

He looks surprised. He says, 'if you're sure'. He suspects he should not believe his luck. You remove your skirt so it does not get creased, and you step in opaque tights into his bed. You pull the duvet up around you. You fuss over pulling it up straight. He follows you, groans indulgently as he reaches the horizontal. You move over to give him space.

It is hot. You hang a foot out in a bid to cool down. Then the other foot. He lies so still that you detect a tremble.

You lie there together.

You are embarrassed to ask anything of him, but there is something you want to know. And so now you too tremble as you speak: 'Maybe you could caress my thigh'. He says again, 'Are you sure?' But then he runs his hands over your legs as though he is kneading dough. He is outside your tights but you feel unprotected, and uncomfortable, and then unsure (as his hands move up to your knickers) where to draw a line—if indeed there is a line still to be drawn.

He is agitated. You do not know to notice the lump behind the zip of his jeans, but you feel his sweat and know he is moving closer. Then his hands leave you and you breathe with relief. He has turned away; his back is to you in the bed and he is leaning on his right elbow, breathing hard and swearing under his breath. He turns back and half-hidden by the flaps of his shirt you recognise a condom pulled shiny and taut.

You are looking past him and up towards the ceiling. You are still. He does not notice. Scrabbling at your waist, he pulls your tights down to your knees and your knickers with them. Then what your logical brain acknowledges must be his penis stubs itself twice against your stomach before, secure, it pushes and twists into your pubic hair. You do not scream or cry out. Instead, eyes closed, you bite your lip, try to focus on something beyond this pain. (You remember your blood being taken in hospital, the prick and the pull of the syringe in your pale, blued skin.)

He moves faster. It hurts more. There is a distinct wave of pain with each shove. It is both sharp and hard, as though your flesh will tear. But still you pull your mind away from it, put your real self in a white room in which you cannot be touched and harmed. Your hands bunch the loose sheets into tight creases and you deliberately breathe relaxation through your clenched teeth into your body.

Then he screams and his penis bobs against you, irregularly, three last times. And his body collapses on top of yours. You are still once more, so still you feel nothing but a cold wetness running into your ears, and you realise his tears are falling onto your face.

In retrospect you are shocked by how violent the movement is.

After a while he sits back on his skinny thighs, and pokes a finger around in your pubic hair. 'There isn't much blood', he says, and you reply, 'Isn't there?'

Lifting himself up he has lifted the duvet with him, and your crumple-clothed body is exposed as he kneels over you. You're a little cold.

'Not really. Some.'

'Oh', you say.

'Did you come?' he says.

'Come? I don't know.' (You do know, but you do not say so. You don't know what it is, but you know it hasn't happened.)

'I'll make you come,' he says, and still kneeling over

your thighs he sticks his finger inside you and moves it vigorously around.

Nothing happens. (It is as though your mind is saving you from something.) But then there is a warmth which begins to interest you. It is a little like a finger coming back to life from being numb with cold. It seems peripheral to what he is doing, to his finger moving forcefully round and in and out. All the same, part of you is starting to feel some sort of pleasure, as though your body were starting to concentrate on one spot. You shift your hips a little to bring the warmth closer to his finger.

You are hardly relaxed, but now you are smiling, beginning to focus your mind on a part of your body you have never noticed before. It is suddenly full of additional life. It demands your attention to an extent that surprises you. But he is tiring. He reaches into you again and hooks his finger out. It is slimy and white. He shows it to you.

'That means you came,' he says. And you say nothing.

Afterwards he sleeps, and you lie there. And that is it. You believe you now know all you needed to know.

But that is not it. That is not and cannot be the end. So take me back to him asleep, his shiny-cheeked smile slackened into quiet formlessness, and to you lying there. How? In the crook of his arm, face nestled to the arm-pit of his shirt? Curled away, a loose spoon in a velveteen box? Face down to the pillows with your thumb in your mouth? Separate, on your back, cold, and with eyes towards a crack on the ceiling?

You don't remember, and your mind now is elsewhere. You wonder whether the combination of your body's resistance and his precipitance means that you are still a virgin. You don't know the answer. And it doesn't matter.

It doesn't matter to you that you've been half-fucked. It

doesn't matter at all. You went along with it because part of you was intrigued. You no longer are. And so you lie there, and nothing matters.

But you're not there now, dear, so I'm going to press you, I'm going to insist you tell me more. Let's start with your statement that it didn't matter. I'm going to push, a little indelicately I'm warning you. (The bane of a writer is to push for the truth.) Which bit didn't matter? The 'half' or the 'fucked'? The fact or its incompetence? Don't you care?

Neither mattered. And you are now once again so far in control of yourself that it hadn't occurred to you that it even should.

When he wakes he washes his hands, and you wash yours though you shake them dry rather than use the mildew-smelling towel, and then he makes toast, slathers it with margarine and you eat it. In the end you do not stay the night.

VIII

That afternoon is the official start of a steady relationship between the two of you, and the fact that you do not care about any aspect of it means your life together is initially easy. During the day he works in a white-blocked office complex on the edge of town while you sleep, or walk in the muddy park. Then in the evenings you turn up and greet him (you have a key to his flat) and you eat together. Often you stay the night.

He is not aware enough to know that this pattern to you is simply what it is, that you are not telling yourself a more complex story about where this has come from, what it means, where it might or might not go from here. (These are all thoughts with which he torments himself.) Nor would he have the sense to hold off if he saw it. He suddenly feels lucky, but as though success is not so glittering as he has been led to expect. Which is to say that it is a long time since he has had a girlfriend, and having one now is more important to him than whether she knows or cares that this is not how it is meant to be. He is disillusioned, but disillusionment is what he has expected.

But, my dear, disillusionment can only support you for so long, and I need to know more than the quick summary you're giving. Let me explain: there could be something else happening here. A girl who has seen the flash of life in migrating geese could be like quicksilver in her boyfriend's life. She could demand colour, activity, and, most of all, excitement. She could suggest cycling out to the country with a picnic in the panniers on the back. She might go dancing and lock her hips to him, laughing, calling his bluff as he claims not to want to dance and she switches her glance to other men. She might spend time dressing up for him. She might also, thinking of the films she has seen, books she has read, the sheer presence of sex in the way the world works, she might reassess whether it might mean more than switching off from a short-lived violence she doesn't understand. I'm not asking you to kit yourself out in black suspenders (though in your position many other girls would), but I do require at least a brief thought of what you are missing out on.

We need to get into all of that stuff, and this is how we're going to do it: you're going to give me some specific examples to work with. I want to see how the two of you function together, what the pattern of spaces and activity is like and what you and he read into that.

Truth be told, I want to know how much I should invest here, and how far I save myself and my words for something later which is more permanent, more worthwhile. I am expert, I hope you agree, in assessing what you say, in understanding how it contributes to the thread of your blossoming post-hospital life. But I need a little more to confirm the angle from which to tell your and Adam's tale.

So, example one: you offer 'A typical evening in the flat'. OK, that will do. Tell me.

It is mid-November, five in the evening, and the sun has already set. You were due to see your doctor this afternoon but have been frozen to this spot. (You took your pills until they ran out, and then your brain sank down a little, but that was all, and that you could cope with.) The sky has passed from streaky red to a bloom of fire-glow and now to winter near-darkness. You are sitting on the bar stool which lives in a corner of Adam's room. Cleared of clothes its varnished surface is sticky and you shift your weight on it with care; the wooden joints are loose and the thought of you being the one whose weight rubs, shudders and jolts them finally apart alarms you in a way you only half acknowledge. (You are fearful both that it is his and that by breaking it you will leave a mark on his world. And yet you are here and you are waiting for him.) With care you have moved it as close as it will go to the window at the back of the room, and you have been looking out through the dusty glass and up, watching the changing colours of the sky. Here it is framed by the foreshortened walls and chimneys of the surrounding buildings. What you see is their back walls and they are windowless and so you struggle to be aware of their height. But what they frame is still enough.

The view you are cricking your neck to watch is a Polaroid print in reverse. At first a colour snapshot, it has become as you watch a piece of film being de-developed, dissolved back into grey-edged shapes with no perspective and then further into simply grey. Now both the moment of beauty and the movie which carried its return to nothingness are done with but you are still sitting there, at once supported and knocked off balance by the now-invisible window which has turned your right cheek numb. By the clock you have been here for a long time, but since it has become dark time has been suspended. And with the lost photograph you too have been taken away from there and opened to something you have always been hiding. Or something even earlier. Now (though you do not put it like this) you are suspended in the space before time and light began, another molecule among millions merely bouncing with varying amounts of energy one against another. You have been turned back to a place with no need for colours or movements or shapes or the relation of shapes to one another.

(Need I say you feel safely alone here, have been alone here for some time, watching the objects around you fade away? But of course that you are most of all waiting for him. You are, aren't you? Remember, this is a scene about you and him. You remember? Good. So tell me.)

The most you can do is notice that you are still breathing: air cooled by the window is coming in through your nose, and that same air, but warmed by your blood, is condensing back onto the glass in front of you. You notice but do not adjust your breath. You do not change your posture to retrieve a clear view of the boxed section of sky which now is only distinguishable from the buildings by an urban orange tinge.

And so you have moved on from waiting to being just here, neither primordial nor contemporary but held in a state of what the meditative traditions call flow. You are holding nothing back and throwing nothing out. And held by this darkness your brain unfurls like a sea anemone in cold dark salt-water. It's OK, a voice tells you, OK for you just to sit and be here. (You listen to the voice and you are silent.) You sit and are suspended and the voice within you takes its roundabout course. You deserve to be hurt, it says, though you do not know what is wrong with you. Life is painful and you need just to do it, to fucking do it and see where it takes you and it's your own fault if you get nothing out. But the sky is beautiful and, fuck everyone else, you can live your own life. (You make no attempt to understand; the place from which this voice comes is not one of understanding.) He is pathetic, the voice tells you. Then, louder, 'you cannot reject him' it says. But his cheeks, you say, are shiny and his penis purple, and you don't get his violence and why it makes him cry. You're broken and broken is what you deserve from the world. Fear. It comes out of the depths like a glove-puppet monster with six-inch claws and you recoil against it though you know it is unreal. Fear. Fear. It tenses you from the heart outwards and locks onto your triceps, locks your throat down against your breathing and pulls your stomach in in nausea. But, no, you have not deserved this.

(Your cheek is still red and numb against the window. You would say, rightly, that you are thinking nothing, but you would be wrong to say your mind is blank. This is a semi-conscious churning of fragments of real thought. You are as though drunk. You have been holding everything inside for months and suddenly you are tired. You don't give a damn, a flying fuck, any-fucking-thing at all. You are irresponsible, you need a break. This is the effect of the fragments in your mind. You can only watch them pass. I can only record them as they were.)

Look! Look at the sky which is fear-filled, which is beautiful, which is lasting, which can make you safe. And then a pod of disgust deep inside you that wants to swell. You know it, you know you are pushing against something that wants to express itself, but which you cannot allow any expression. Why? You ask why? Because the monster will come and destroy it all, the beast will arise out of the depths and then there will be no more you, and no more darkness and just a swelling, growing, burning sickness that tears across the land, that holds the sky dark when light should come, that pulls everything in its wake until it churns in a sea the colour of treacle and grasping like treacle to drown you to its depths. Because you are hated, lost and hated and deserving of no man's pity or help or sanity or kindness. All you deserve is pain. You need to hold yourself back. You need to destroy whatever in you pulls you towards those depths from which you can never emerge and in which you are though the world and he see something else. You are drowning, drowning and the world does not know or care.

And you are on the point of tears, about to break a path through into what you know will be the truth of who you are, to acknowledge with a physical reaction in time what, out of time, your mind is holding closest to you. You are about to feel what it is that is binding your energy away from your consciousness; you are about to open the gates to feeling, however inappropriate that feeling may be. And then—you recognise the noise—a key scrapes in the lock.

The monster is waking, is stretching its claws and reaching out for your heart; it will tear you, score your skin six inches deep; its breath will burn you until there is no more you to burn.

But already the key is turned, the door is open and—tick—Adam has switched on the lights. At the sound you have turned around too fast, have pulled your face too abruptly out of another world, and as you create a smile to welcome him home your throat is raw against a burp of acid which you cannot swallow down.

Adam does not see the strain on your bloodless face, does not notice the shift of emotion that has just taken place in his room. Instead he takes four quick steps across the carpet and, blinking, you reach your bare toes down and tip your weight off the stool towards him. It creaks. You receive the perfunctory kiss. He is still carrying the excitement which has propelled him back from work earlier than usual. He says, 'My parents want to invite us for Christmas. We can do that, can't we?'

He rolls the word 'we' with pleasure on his tongue. You look at him and then around the room. It is as though the walls have changed their temperature and with that their colour and you are out of place again. All you deserve is pain and he is waiting, open-mouthed, for your answer. The ceiling is cobwebbed in the corners and you have not yet remembered to brush the dust off the singed lampshade. The monster has claws but they are dissolving into the light. The bar stool is a battered yellowed pine.

'I suppose so, yes,' you answer.

'Are you sure?' he asks.

And you answer again, 'yes, that's fine.'

But something else is happening as you answer, something much more important. He expects more of you than a simple assent. You know it. You see it in his now-blinking pause—the fish-like look he has when he wants to take you to bed—, in the hesitation which has already become his embarrassment. You know it and you are conscious in your refusal to give it. Notice this. This is something new for you, and it is something momentous. It is both created and masked by the vestige of the other world which has retained its grip on part of your mind. It is unkind, but it is yours; your musing has taken you far away and you have returned here by a slightly different route.

You both stand there in the middle of the room, with the red mark from the window on your cheek as though someone has slapped you. You begin to cry. Adam takes you in his arms and, reassured, he whispers, 'I love you.'

You stand there together, his arms around you.

(Or was it the other way round? Did he tell you he loved you and then you began to cry? You refuse to answer me. Your face is cold. It did not matter, you tell me. All that matters is that you were alone with the sky and then you were switched back to being with him and then the sky was gone.)

End of example, you say.

And I for one am unsatisfied. Not that you have told me only about yourself. I did not expect you to talk about him; I've learned by now that it's not your way. I do not condone it in the slightest—you promised me a romantic tale to write—but I do recognise that currently you are in transition from alone to together, and that self-centredness is still the way you are. That characteristic will not make you into a good wife. But we are not yet at that stage, and we will still save you for the heroine of our tale. We can shelve that worry for later.

More problematic is that your example was short on meat. That is to say it was thin. No 'buts', my dear. Pay attention. You must remember that though all you see is my sympathy—another cup of tea, perhaps?—my mind in the background is shaping our art, building the architecture that will show the beauty of your tale. And what I say is that there is no narrative flow of the inevitable; I don't know how you get from there to here. You've said too little for me to tell. But that is not a problem: we need merely take another example. You look up and you nod. Christmas perhaps, I suggest, and you nod again. It was pivotal, you say, and you shudder as you say the word, and I see that your eyes are pleading. So let us take that: it is good to take a time which really matters, and at the least it follows on naturally. I think I even just saw a blush.

You ask to start by telling me something that you only knew later. I permit you this diversion. You say this: that the joint celebration of Christmas this year was something new in Adam's family. He has not, you say, had Christmas at home since he left at sixteen. You say you need that acknowledged to prove that what happened was equally false, equally some sort of anomaly. OK. I get that you have a reading of this situation which you wish to have heard. (I am intrigued.) I recognise that you wanting to shape your story is a sign you are taking some control of your life. I should welcome that; I do. Just remember that in the terms of our contract I have the final artistic rights, and I put forward that maybe it is simpler than you claim, maybe you need not be so dismissive; maybe all that will happen is that the four of you will share a celebratory meal. We will see, I say confidentially, and you blush again. Both your hands rock irregularly from side to side.

Christmas Day? I ask, and you assent. Christmas Day. Twelve noon.

The scene: the unused front room of a small terraced house.

The cast: you, Adam, his parents. (Adam has not told you their names, and so let them be 'he' and 'she'.) You, he and Adam are drinking cut-glass thimbles of warm sherry. She is not present. She is in the kitchen.

Adam is talking. He is saying that it's one of those cold grey-green sorts of Christmases, but better that way than a slushy one. Adam's father is silent. He is looking out of the window, his face as blank and content as that of an inmate of a nursing-home. Adam continues. He says that when you left home yesterday it was actually quite warm. You have nothing to say and so you do not respond. Nor does his father. (You are thinking that Adam's voice is louder than usual, but then you think that since that first conversation in your hall his penchant with you has been for sweet nothings *sotto voce*, and that you would not know how he normally speaks.) Adam turns to you and hopes you are warm enough. You nod. You say, 'yes, fine', and he blinks.

His father stands to a stoop, crosses the room, bends himself further to switch the portable bar-heater on at the plug, then sits back down.

The three of you sit as though you are in a museum, as though you are required to study, with concentration, the beaded antimacassars, the pale imitation Wedgwood balanced on the dark dresser, the silver-framed black and white photo of somebody's wedding party. Into the silence comes the ringing of the egg-timer and then the gusty sound of the oven overlaid with the dull crump of buckling roasting tins. Adam says again how nice it is to be here. There still is no response. (Your heart, you are surprised, contracts for him.) Then he too is silent.

You sit, and you avoid each others' eyes. Adam is watching the changing view of his shoes as he crosses and re-crosses his ankles. His face is red. You are looking at the dents in the carpet which show you the dining table has been pulled out from its space by the wall. It has also been extended with a leaf that is a darker wood than the rest and the whole is flamboyantly over-set with silver paper and candles, as though she has made an effort without knowing (beyond effort) what she wants it to convey. A sprig of holly stands proud in a ring of candles in the middle and it is already going brown. You feel a pang of delicacy towards her though she is yet to show any warmth to you. Once more you are surprised at yourself.

Your thoughts drift on in the silence. Someone, you think, has used this parti-coloured table before, but surely it was not these people here, who are all the wrong size and shape to be together in the room. Because suddenly the room is crowded: the woman is trotting in and out, her arms webbed with the two-handed oven-glove, and she is leaning over heavy pottery dishes, blinded by the steam that rises from them and onto her glasses; the old man sits still in a crumpled silence as though his body has been emptied to fill the bulging flock cushions that make him seem so small; the younger man, shiny-faced, is now shifting and shuffling again, is commenting on how long a journey he has taken to be here, is reciting to his father the reviews of the book he has bought and which he knows will sit here unread.

You all sit down to the table without an attempt at joy. (You shuffle to your places one by one as though nothing special is happening, as though there is no reason to be here.) No-one admits that the cooking has been mistimed, that the roast potatoes crunch translucent on the inside, that the turkey is dry and tough, that the sprouts have turned to mush. No-one comments that a proper Christmas dinner has not been eaten in this house for many years. Nonetheless, Adam is revived by the wine and the increasing heat of the room. He is talking more fluently again. (Under the table he is running his heavy-shoed foot up and down your new pair of tights. You push away your irritation that they must be being laddered.)

'You so wanted to come for Christmas, didn't you, darling?' he says. 'And clearly you weren't going to come to us.'

You realise Adam has decided that after all there is a battle to be fought here, and that you are silent artillery for him to push from side to side. His mother says nothing. She is as though concentrating on every mouthful, pausing every so often only to tuck her dark-dyed pudding bowl haircut back behind her ears.

'Rachel wanted to be with me to celebrate,' he says, and you, self-conscious, say nothing.

He is nonetheless intent on showing off that he is loved:

'Next year we'll host Christmas, won't we darling? I reckon that we can do this.'

From mere hesitation, and then painful smugness, his jollity has developed a hard jeering note. Let us give him credit; he is locked too far in his protective self to realise this. But you see his father stop chewing and look down, and his mother pauses with her fork half-way to her mouth and she says, 'Well.' She says, 'Happy for you. Happy.' As she speaks her voice first wavers and then goes quiet. The four of you chew round and round at the turkey. Almost in unison you sip the wine.

In turn you clear your plates, and though there is no sense of transition you find yourselves in the pause after the main course. The mother is in the kitchen extricating the pudding from its scalding steam. The father is looking again towards the window. Adam pushes back his chair and walks out of the room. You sit alone with his father.

Then Adam calls you: 'Rachel, just come here a minute, can you?' And this, it seems, is the moment that he has decided the day has been saving itself for. The sparseness of the celebration so far has made it inevitable that as you step into the hall he should kiss you in a sudden determined vision of precipitate romanticism. And maybe it is also inevitable that you put your arms around him and respond. Maybe this is how you are feeling his mother's pain. Maybe you are searching for a human warmth to justify the attempt at the Christmas ideal. Maybe you don't want to make a fuss, a noise, with only a thin wall between the two of you and each of his now-discomfited parents.

Whatever the reason, your mouth is tight at how inappropriate his sudden show of desire is. But then it slackens against his. With a rare gift for timing he has chosen this moment to try a new move; here, between courses in the dark narrow hall he has felt through your sweater for both of your nipples and is pinching and twisting them hard.

(You remind me that you are warm with sherry and wine, that you are trapped against the wall, that you have no-one to call on, nowhere to go.)

You remind me of that because this moment is, despite yourself, overcoming your disgust. You have wanted to hold yourself apart. You have wanted to be dependent on no-one. Yet what you feel now is not only a piquing level of physical desire which you can enjoy and watch from a distance, alone. What you feel is a compulsion to erase your brain in proximity to, as part of, him. Let us assume that part of you wants simply to give in and be overwhelmed so you can escape the hot embarrassment of being turned on in his parents' hall. Maybe. But what you want most is a sharper, harder, deeper feeling, and you are pressing your body to his, suddenly not only wanting but also trusting his instinct to give it to you.

You are being pleasured. You know that. But more importantly you are surprised and grateful to whatever god there may be that on this of all days you can feel this, be part of this, come together with him to create this whole. It is this gratefulness which blossoms into a tremor of understanding, and as your mouth pulls away you feel your perception opened on a different world. Without thinking you whisper that you love him.

Let us be clear: 'I love you' is what you say.

His intake of breath takes your breath from you, and then as he twists a final time you take that breath back again into your lungs. You shiver. He is shaking. For a moment you are together in a world which is focused tight on the two of you. And then you hear plates being stacked in the kitchen and you are there, hot and hand-in-hand in the hall and it is time to eat the pudding.

Adam is high. He insists that the pudding must be lit. She goes back again to the kitchen. 'It's been used for the cake', she says as she hands the bottle over. She has caught in Adam's face the face of her boy, and anticipation awakens in her despite herself.

'For libation,' says Adam's father, now also watching as Adam slops it, and slops it again. You too watch. You are conscious that you are present with Adam's parents, but you also now believe in a version of this room which is more gorgeous and vibrant, into which, shimmering, you and Adam have stepped. You think to yourself that they are the audience and they are applauding, worshipping you both. You are thinking that this meal is a transition point for you. Sitting at the table you are open to feeling as you have never been before. The flame jumps its shiver of blue from the plate to the top of the sticky dome and down and round, an effervescence that races over a solid reality. Your mind has become receptive to everything any metaphor can make of it. But in fact the four of you are already a little disappointed: the flicker is practically instantaneous, over before anyone thinks to turn out the lights, and all it leaves on the pudding is a taste with no strength.

Nonetheless, that night Adam offers to try to make you come. You say, 'no, not to worry,' so he pushes your head with both hands down to his crotch, and then, satisfied, he falls asleep.

You do not sleep. You are considering your enlarged perception alone. You feel ridiculous. Like the flame it has thinned until it is nothing. You are ashamed. You shift away from Adam's hot body beside you. The warmth you felt over lunch is no longer there and when you think about it nor do you expect it to be. And so you lie, and while Adam snores you complete your retreat from him.

End of example, you say, and you look at me with a defiant expectation.

And it's true: I'm interested, happy to take on the baton here. You think that he is nothing to you, and yet you meant it when you said you loved him. No, you say, it was merely lust and you mistook its meaning. You insist. You say there was never love, only a double warmth of alcohol and sex. But it's more than that, I tell you. (I have seen this before.) Your body was warmed up, I grant you, but so was your mind. However briefly, you were absorbed into him, including through your mind. If that is not love then I do not know what is.

OK, you're frightened as a result. You feel alarmed at the position your confession has put you in. You are not sure yet you want to settle down; marriage for you is not yet top of mind. But a bit of alarm is normal. You'll get used to the prospect. Ultimately it will be good for you.

You say no. Your voice is firmer. You say you do not care about Adam or about anything else, and that you are certainly not on the edge of marriage. You are retreating even from me as you say it; you have pulled up your knees and wrapped your arms around them, and your hair has fallen across your eyes. I agree (I have to) that there is evidence to suggest that this detachment is true. But it is not true all of the time, and you are recovering, growing further away from your self-centredness and into a more caring world. Think about it, even from the start you have cared. From the start you have not held back the whole of your response. Like when you shook and panicked on the bus home, like (yes, I mention it) when Peter did not come. See—I can tell from your reaction now, from your thrown back head, from that sudden squint in your eyes and your twisted mouth, I can see there is still something inside that can feel, something inside you that hurts.

So, let us be clear: you love him, and you have told him so. I want to know what happens next.

All right, you say. All right. And there is a hard, focused look in your eyes. You say you will tell me what happened next. Another celebration, you say, and your face twists again, and its sudden redness is anger not a maiden blush. (Now it is my turn to be alarmed.) You agreed, you say, to tell my story. So example three: your birthday with his friends.

I take your offering; it is what I must do. Your Birthday with His Friends.

It is April 21st and flags are hung out to celebrate the Queen's birthday, and you, you say, are also on formal duty, on public display. You are in the cheap café round the corner from Adam's office. You, Adam, and two colleagues of his you have never heard of before. They are called Richard and Moira.

(You say, defiantly, that they have taken pity on him, and that is the only reason they are here. I tell you to tell the story, not to pre-empt my interpretation of what it means. You continue.)

And actually we discover straight-away that you are wrong. You are, it seems, an add-on to what you have never known is a daily lunch routine. Richard, Moira, Adam; they are greeted by name by the waitress and need only nod for their orders to be placed. You in turn choose ham and grated cheese with pickle on white.

'And I'll have a beer,' Adam announces. 'It's a celebration.'

The four of you sit down at a table in the corner.

'So, this is Rachel', Adam says, and he waves his hand at you as though you were a rabbit emerging from a hat. 'Richard, Moira: Rachel. We work together. How long is it now? Three years nearly? That about right?'

Both Richard and Moira say yes, that's right, and how good it is to meet you, how they've heard so much. You nod. You smile. There is a pause. You shift on your chair. You look up towards the corner of the room. You look down. (There is, you say, something pulling hard inside you and which you want to hide. I say, no; you do not need to hide. I say that instead you are doing something normal. You are worried that his friends might not like you, worried about how you may come across. You are shy. But I applaud you; this is within the bounds of reasonable anticipation.)

'Hi,' you say, 'great to meet you too.'

'Just over here for lunch,' says Adam. 'But not too far for you to come, eh, love?'

'No,' you say. 'Twenty minutes. Maybe twenty-five.'

'Oh, yes,' Moira says.

And Richard says, 'So not too far.'

There is another pause which is interrupted by the arrival of the sandwiches which you all shuffle round the table, making room.

'And where've you come from Rachel? What do you do?'

'I'm between jobs,' you say. (You've thought this one out.) Moira is silent. Then 'ah' she says, and bites into her sandwich and mayonnaise squeezes out at the side of her mouth.

She chews, and as if that's a sign you all start to eat. Between bites both Richard and Moira smile genially towards you, but when Adam starts a conversation about work they join in with what looks like relief. Occasionally they glance at you for a view, and you nod, you say that what they do sounds complicated, that it must be interesting. You mean no such thing. But no-one, it seems, wants really to talk to you or has anything to say about your birthday, and no-one feels discomfort at that. You are also comfortable: the lunch is fulfilling your expectations, requiring nothing of you, allowing you what has become your protective disdain.

But there comes a point when Adam and Moira are deep in shared work and Richard has turned to talk directly to you, and you find that despite yourself you are talking back to him and that you are interested. He is, he announces, training his bulk for a marathon. That is the phrase he uses, 'training my bulk'. He puts his hand on yours on the table (on the one that Adam has left free). He says, 'Go on, say it. Tell me what a fatty I am. Tell me it's all no use.' And he laughs at himself. 'No, no,' you say, and he laughs again.

'Yes, yes, you're thinking it,' he says. 'Good for me, though. All those early mornings, thumping miles out round the streets. I'm feeling better than I have done for years.'

And then despite yourself you are looking curiously at him. There is a softness in his face which intrigues you. It is mobile but with fluidity and not the abruptness you see in Adam and feel in yourself. And he does not look away or tighten his eyes against your gaze. Instead he smiles, and he pats your hand and he lets it go. 'There's a way to go,' he says, 'you're right about that. But I'm getting there and I'm dreaming of a cold beer at that finishing line.'

(What you are seeing in Richard is authenticity, though all you know is that it is something new.)

'I'll tell you what,' he says, 'you should get this lad onto it. Get rid of that wan look he has. Use your feminine influence. Catch him when he's in the bath contemplating his paunch and give him a nudge then.' And, friendly, he hits Adam between his shoulders.

Adam looks at you, eyes dilated with sudden fear, and you are ashamed for his self-consciousness as well as for yourself. So of course you smile, and of course you return Adam's squeezes, but still you are talking to Richard and wishing you were unencumbered. It is not that you are attracted to him. Let us be clear: it is that you are ashamed by the assumption that you have influence over this Gollum of a man. (Your first impression is suddenly perched again at the top of your mind.) The shame is that Richard, happily-married, assumes that your relationship is also true, is moving towards the permanency of marriage and children, is underlaid by a pragmatic but intimate love. Before his sincerity you are humiliated by what your taste must seem to be, then by fear that they are wondering how you must behave with him, what you are like in bed together.

You pull your hand away from Adam's.

'Everything alright, darling?' he asks. You blush, at his words and at the assumption that he is your keeper, and then at the reasonableness of that assumption; and there is a silence.

Richard breaks it, looking at his watch: 'Right chaps,' he says, 'I need to head. Need to get back to the desk.' He stands up. 'Come again and say hello,' he says. 'Good to meet you—we've heard so much. You've changed this man's life.' His hand is suddenly protective on Adam's shoulder.

You say again, 'no, no'. But as though performing a duty you clasp Adam's hand and look up at him, and he smiles proudly back down to you like a schoolboy who has just won a prize. You feel perversely as though you have achieved something too, though you do not know what.

'I need to get back too,' says Moira, and she also stands and shakes herself out ready to leave.

And Adam says, 'I'll be with you in five.'

'Of course,' Richard says, 'give the birthday girl a goodbye kiss.'

You want to be repelled. But the laugh he laughs again as he lumbers across the café is warm and kind, and, still kindly, he ushers Moira out of the door.

You reverse Adam's attempt at a kiss into a hug, say that you're sure he must be getting back, and you get up and you walk out of the door.

That's it, you say. End of example. You are defiant. Closed.

That perturbs me. And—let me put it bluntly—I'm also confused. For you say that this relationship, that Adam, means nothing and, what's more, it (and he) will mean nothing. But you have also said you love him, you are performing social duties at his side, you are allowing his and others' assumptions to flourish. If I didn't know you better I'd say that this is duplicitous, but let me try to presume the best. That best, and please don't cry, my dear, is that you are lost and confused. (You nod and your face opens with relief.) So let me elucidate, let me help. This is what happens as time goes on: the initial excitement of feeling in love (of feeling it in your every fibre and in his every glance) settles into merely love. You come to the stage where some days are wonderful, but others are humdrum, just so. That is where you are now: your birthday lunch was clearly not a triumph, but nor did it close any doors. You should not be ecstatic, I agree, but nor was anything wrong.

So let us start instead from there: you are still frightened by the intimacy of being in love, frightened by the different shape it gives to you, frightened by its presence in the day-to-day, and you are pushing against that with teenage rebellion, trying both to find the boundaries and to establish your comfort against them.

OK: on that basis I am prepared to continue. Carry on. Tell me where this goes next.

You smile at me grimly, and you say you will.

IX

It is a month later; it is May; it is Thursday.

It is the first day that the sun has made it down to Adam's patio and you are sitting out there on a plastic bag stretched across the seat of the rotting wooden bench. Adam is in the room behind you, standing at the stove. He is boiling dried pasta; you hear the hiss of the water on the solid hob. You are wondering what to do with a secret that you have, a secret you have held separate in your mind for some weeks now. It is very simple and it is practical. (And, no, you are not pregnant.) Your secret is this: your lease on your flat runs out next week (as finally do the pre-hospital savings in your bank account) and without reflecting on it openly you have neither told Adam nor thought at all about what happens next. It is as though the end of the world is upon you but it is merely bureaucratic and nothing in you can be brought to care. You sit, and you contemplate that fact, separate from Adam as he prepares your dinner behind you.

Your flat is your own, says the beating bass note. Bare of belongings, it has housed your mind in privacy since you were discharged. Without discussing it you have lived your life with Adam solely on the ground floor, solely in the darkness of his studio rather than in your first-floor temple to the dawn. And that temple is still there, says your jumping heart, the view is seen each day by the pale blank walls though you are only ever there when the day has arrived and Adam has left for work. That pale room has been a haven you have retreated to alone. But it is going to be destroyed, and as yet you have nothing to put in its place.

You look at the patio around you, and despite everything the light here is beautiful. It picks out the roughness of the brick walls as though it is carefully-quarried stone. The ivy is no longer dank and throws elegant shadows across the wall; and the paving stones are dry for the first time since October. You sit, and now you are calm. You have been here for nearly an hour. Your arms are on the point of stretching out and your shoulders have relaxed enough to let a smile grow on your pale face. This expansion feels natural, as though it is something you have done before, but that this time you mean it. Let me say again that you are content.

So when Adam calls you inside to eat, calls you away from the light, you are annoyed. You feel your annoyance as a sharp tightness which is directed against him. And then your chest turns to concrete and you realise that your contentedness can only sit with the thought that you will no longer be here.

You walk inside and say: 'I don't want to be with you anymore.'

Adam is standing by the slab of veneered chipboard work-surface. He flushes a dark, dark pink, and he puts the pan of pasta and sauce back down on the cooling hob. He starts to shake.

He says nothing.

And so after a pause you try again: 'I'm sorry,' you say, 'but it's not going to work.' (You have heard this phrase somewhere before.)

His hands are clasped into fists and tears are gathering in a row along the line of his jaw.

You are not afraid; you do not respect what he is feeling as real. Nor do you expect it to be transmitted to you. You are cut off, holding to yourself the sense of your self unfurled, floating above him, on the first floor and watching the dawn. You smell the harsh smell of pesto like vomit on the air. You think he should get himself under control.

'You need to take that pan off the hob,' you say.

'Fuck the pan.'

And you say, 'come on, be reasonable, please take the pan off the hot hob.' You smile in a way you intend as kind and encouraging.

'What's happened?' he asks, and as you watch he bangs his fists impotently together. 'What have I done? What the fuck have I done?'

You say nothing. You cannot explain it is nothing to do with anything he has or has not done.

He says, 'What do you mean it's not going to work?'

You do not answer.

He becomes more harsh: 'You jumped pretty fast into bed with me, didn't you?'

Your face loses its contours as you stifle any reaction. You do not recognise the justness of his remark. The story you have told yourself is that he seduced you. You believe, though you do not quite say this to yourself, that he has obscurely taken advantage of you, of your vulnerability, of your virginity. It does not occur to you that his anger is disappointment and fear. You see just unjustified anger, and so you observe it. It gives you an excuse for distance.

'You promised we'd be together. You told me you loved me.' He spreads his hands against the wall behind him, presses his anger into it. He is vindictively aware that their wetness will damage the paper and mark this moment in the fabric of his life. 'I've told my parents—told them we'll be married. They're waiting for us to set a date.'

Even you know this is ridiculous, not the way it is meant to be. Your excuse grows. But he does not see that your decision is permanent (its sudden permanence is surprising you as well), that already you are peering disdainful at his uncontrolled emotion from behind a supercilious smile you think is kindness.

'I'm sorry. I'm sorry but it's not going to work.' You pause. Something stirs in your abdomen and you swallow it down fast to retain your control. You are suddenly bigger than he is, aware that this is not what love should be like, aware that this relationship has been a farce. Something has jolted you into another phase of your life and you are already looking back at Adam as the past. You do not say this to him either. Instead you say, 'Come here, come here, don't cry'. You hold back the urge to say 'darling, darling, don't cry'. You pull his head in to your chest as though he were a child, but as his hand comes to your breast you push it away.

'No, not that. Now, don't cry, honey. Baby, don't cry.' For a moment your generous composure is threatened; he is forcing his hand up inside your jumper, you are handling it down with motherly tones. 'No, don't do that. Try not to do that.' Then he pulls away in a shudder of urgency, as if to stay were to force himself on you. His wet inarticulacy turns to sobs on the bed, and you stand up, walk across the room, and transfer the pan to a cold ring of the hob. Then you cross the room again, open the door and step through it. You pull it silently closed with a heartfelt wish for him to have a good night.

You are calm as you tell me all of this. Rationally you have retained the high ground. You are perplexed at the swell of his feeling. But you are pleased you have learned to cope so well, that you can be the wise one, that you are old beyond your years.

But though you are calm as you leave Adam to sob for his lost chance at marriage, for the fact that he will never have children, for the fact, as well, that he will be lonely, poor and dirty in old age, that other people's children will cross the street to avoid him (he is sobbing all of this out aloud to himself), you still feel obscurely that there is something wrong in you. You turn a harsh eye on his self-indulgent loss of control but your rational control is not bringing you comfort either. And so rather than turning up the stairs to your flat you tell yourself (as you would have told him) that a walk will do you good.

You come out of the flats and turn away from town. Your instinct is to take yourself away from the world. So you turn left not right. Not, you tell me, that it matters either way. And you look discomfited as you say that, with a furrow in your forehead and a tight bulge of muscle either side of your jaw.

So tell me, tell me about your walk.

(You look at me as though I am a fool.)

You set off, you say, Adam's tears still wet on your hands. You are distracted and uncomfortable and you want to push that away, overcome it, take it out of your life. Your feet strike the pavement on the left and right in a determinedly precise rhythm, and you feel your weight rock on each side from heel to toe as though you are a puppet with a string for each joint. All your concentration is on the consistency of this motion: heel to toe, left then right. The movement is switching you off from your feeling, allowing your mind to build a floodwall that strengthens the permanence of your break-up. (The darkness in your mind is shame and fear; the wall you are building is to hold it back with every ounce of effort you have.)

At first, despite your effort, you are moving slowly. Your feet are tentative; you struggle with the effort of putting them down. (Your mind is being threatened by the pressure of the darkness.) But gradually you feel them more securely on the ground and your muscles slip into a rhythm and the messages flow securely to and from your brain. Your mind's defences strengthen. Your shoulders, too, relax and as your chest opens out you breathe deeply and your chin comes up. You start to look around you.

Although by this time of year it is light in the evenings this area is empty and quiet. The roadside here has no houses or shops so what traffic there is comes past at speed, with no reason to slow or stop. Your mind is undisturbed by the passing cars. The rhythm of your walk is becoming automatic, and that safety is allowing a set of thoughts to flow: you are glad that you held to yourself that the lease is ending on your flat—he will not be able to find you, you think, you will run away, leave him, leave this place. The breeze blows coolly on your uncovered arms which swing to and fro with your martial feet. You are congratulating yourself on your achievement. You have, you say, the strength to move away now, you know who you are, and you are a rational adult where he is an indulgent child. Part of you is ashamed, but you are right despite your shame. You walk on, following the road as it curves round and heads into another part of town. The odd side road branches off, but the land remains still and open around you. It is calming, and it is quiet.

It is the quietness which means you notice there is a man walking towards you. You see him first when he is three lamp posts away. (He is on your side of the road.) You are more relaxed than you were, but something still is biting at the edges of your mind, part of you is still focused on holding something back. The presence of this man triggers shots of adrenalin leaping into that fear, linking it back again through to where you are now. And so you observe him with care. You see he is unwashed, and that he is drunk. His face is the veined taupe of his sandy-red hair; only the texture is different, drawing your eyes down even at this distance from haze-edged matte to clearly-rounded shininess. He is carrying a weighty plastic bag, its handles pulled tight and twisted so they lock the blood out of his hand.

You walk on.

But now he is two lamp posts away and despite the hold you have gained on your mind your body is flickering into automatic alarm. The dark pool you were beginning to still is suddenly violently choppy: fear is jerking up from your stomach, through your neck, down to your hands which have clasped together without you realising it. You slow your pace, begin to look around. And as you slow he stops and he stands there as though he has forgotten something and is debating whether to go back, or as though some memory pains him so much he needs to wait while physically it racks through him from head to toe. You slow your pace further, begin to lose the solidity which you were gaining from your walk, begin to watch the traffic for a gap to cross the road. Your body is braced as though you have received a firm warning of impending harm. He is still those two lamp posts away; there is, you tell yourself, no reason you should feel this alarm. But you do. It is real.

You half-watch, your eyes glancing to check you are safe, and up again to find the gap to cross the road. He is still standing, and then as you watch him he drops his bag as though hit by an electric shock, and it sags slowly over the kerb edge. Stiffly he hobbles from one foot to the other—left to right, with a stutter, and right to left again. You are struck by a feeling like conscience which tells you that you should move forward and help (that this is what a heart-attack looks like); but nothing of you can emerge from the bubble of fear which encloses you, so you stay still. The car that is passing sounds its horn, briefly and then held firmly down. You see his hands come up to his chest as he pirouettes back and forth, narrowly missing tipping into the road. You yourself step into the road, cross it half at a run and then carry on walking faster towards the houses that are on the next corner. Horns are sounding behind your back. You break into a half-run, then slow and try deliberately to steady your breathing, try as well to look unconcerned, to look as though you have noticed nothing, as though as far as you know there has been nothing to see. (If anyone asks then you will tell them you are deaf.) But with that you have a sudden fear that you have seen a man die, and a sob which is a deep scream rises in your throat. You swallow it down.

And now you feel that you are only tentatively touching the ground, that you may be pulled up and away, asymmetrical, broken and that no-one will warn you when the moment will come. Except that like a puppet you have no real sensation, only the fact that all you are is taken up again with concentration on walking.

Round the corner as the houses begin again you reach a bench and sit down. The jerks through your body are weakening. You are shivering, but you are succeeding in closing yourself off again from the world. You do not hear the sirens arrive but when they come you begin to cry. You believe you are crying for the man who died in the road. But then you are also crying for yourself, crying that no-one is there to help or to comfort you, and crying from the release of destroying Adam's life.

You have to walk back to your flat by the same route. There is now no traffic, a complete stillness under the street lamps. By one of them you see in the gutter a plastic bag, a dented tin of tuna and a pint of milk, burst by the black rubber mark which has shrieked across the road. You walk on slightly faster, acknowledging nothing to yourself of the fear that twists in your gut. You reach your building, unlock the outside door as close to silently as you can. Then, on the threshold, you glance back into the street behind you and you notice something which makes you stop. You tense back your knees to hold your puppet feet heavily on the ground and you watch a girl walking casually down the street. She is young and beautiful, in careless tracksuit separates, one hand twiddling the drawstring of her hood as she chatters on her phone. But what strikes you most is her candy-floss-pink hair.

And that, you tell me, is how you decide. How you know what the next thing is for you to do. You say it hits you with a greater reality than any of Adam's pain. You say that the place you need is by the sea.

X

Then it is simple. The next morning at dawn you close your door behind you, push the keys and a note through the letter box, then take a taxi from the corner of the street to the station. You leave with the two suitcases that are all you own on the seven a.m. train. At first you go to Manchester Piccadilly and then you go south to the end of the line, and where you end up is Bournemouth. You arrive in the early afternoon. You place your suitcases in the station left luggage as though you are an adult woman displaying purpose and sense. Then, unencumbered, you emerge from the shadow of the multi-storey car-park and latch onto clear brown signs which say 'Beaches and Pier'.

You need the signs. The station is in a grubby part of town, the wide streets lined with fast food joints, betting shops, off-licences and nail bars. (There is none of the glory you had hoped to see. There is no sign of the sea.) You continue to follow the signs, emerging from an underpass, crossing several roundabouts, passing the Spiritualist church and then the Baptist one. Then the road tips down a hill lined with blocks of flats, with stunted palms growing between the carriageways, and at the end beyond a large white turreted building that must be a hotel is the promised flat expanse of the sea.

Your pace quickens. You pass more flats, a Mexican sit-down restaurant, an Italian, the YMCA, and the white turrets resolve themselves into the Royal Bath Hotel. You pass it, too. And then the car parks, and still following the signs you thread through the concrete pillars of the main road which you are surprised is raised above you, and you emerge between the Pavilion and the carriageway, and some restaurants and the pier.

You stop, and you stand. There is no smell here of the sea, no haunting scream of gulls. You stand in surprise for a moment. Then you turn your head slowly from one side to the other. And as you do you draw in your breath. For though where you are is ugly and dirty and loud, though there is litter and you can smell the cars, and there is graffiti on the concrete pillars; for though that is what you are in, either side of you is something different. Either side of the pier the beach stretches out wide and cream-coloured until in the far distance it is gathered in by the misty curve of the cliffs. You turn to the right and walk along the flat tarmac that edges the beach almost at the level of the sea. You reach a bench, sheltered from the wind by a plastic hoarding advertising the town. You lean your hip against it, and you watch.

You are no longer disappointed.

The tide is in. Spray fans up and onto the pier, shocking the tourists who despite the cold day are standing within the sea's reach of the rail. They brush themselves down, but look over into the water again and again, smiling, laughing, shaking their skirts dry. And at beach-level too the world is being recreated. You stand in the breeze and you watch, and you see the genesis of each new wave, the swell growing, thinning, whitening, breaking in a pattern which slowly grows into your blood as in a bigger rhythm the waves too arrive at several feet in height and then start once again at the gentlest ripple. Salt dries roughly on your face. You stand, wrapped in your scarf, and you look out to sea; and you breathe slowly in and out: something in you is lighter than it has been.

You notice none of the people walking along the

waterfront. You are absorbed in the flux of the repeated birth of nothing. But one of them has noticed you. A middle-aged gentleman whose brown mackintosh collar is raised against the wind, who was sitting on the next bench down before you arrived and has waited much longer than he had expected, having told himself he would watch to see your blot of colour go. Eventually you turn, and he sees your young face reddened from the salt and the wind, and despite it all he smiles, and he, too, feels lighter than he has been.

THE SEA

I

You turn parallel to the sea and walk another few yards along the tarmac. You push open the door of the white-painted café. Your voice is clear as you order 'tea, no, just the tea, yes, with milk'. You sit, and you sip, and the steam from your cup condenses to wetness on your cheeks. You wrap your stiff fingers around the china. Your eyes too focus on this captured warmth, as though they too could drink it in. You sit. Time passes and what you feel is relief. There is nothing you need do, no-one to hide from or for whom you need prepare a public face. You can drift on the remembered rhythm of the waves whose regular spray you still see, blurred, through the steamed-up window glass.

The shop around you is quiet; it is Friday and the season has only just begun. For the first time in months you feel at peace. Already only semi-conscious, you are further lulled by the voices around you. Two voices, one a deep-toned, sighing drawl and the other a fast light patter.

'And you're still on for Sunday?' says the drawl to the patter, and the patter replies, 'Yes, yes. I checked with Mum. Her boyfriend's coming round so I'm better off out.'

China clinks, and then the scratchy sound of metal tins being roughly stacked. You recognise the sounds and as you follow them across the air you feel as though you are gradually opening out, as though your range is being extended. The image of a sea anemone passes through your mind attached to nothing you know.

'How's that going?' says the deeper drawl. 'You like him?'

'Yeah, I like him well enough. Doesn't have much to say

to me. He's like "hello Jen" and pats me on the back then he's with her. He's OK.'

'Not your Dad, hey hon.'

'No-one's Dad.'

The door opens and bangs shut pushing a pillow of cold air through the room.

'A filter coffee to take out? Certainly, madam. Sugar? No? Be careful, it's hot. Just what you need on a day like today. There you are.'

'Thank you. Thank you.'

'Have a good one. Goodbye.'

Another pillow of air bulges as far as the corner where you sit.

'Can't close the bloody door, can she,' says the drawl and you hear quick footsteps across the tiles and the sound of the waves is dulled again.

'God, should be ice-cream by this time of year,' she says, 'but they're saying it's better from the end of the week. Low twenties, they're saying,' and on she talks: what more could we hope for this early on, and the families are starting to appear, for the day right now but the holidays start in a couple of weeks and then it'll be the usual riot, odd last year, that hot spell in April and nothing then till June, but they'd all pre-booked, almost better, then, if the weather's not great, wouldn't wish it on them, of course—no good in the long run—but a bit of a breeze and then they come in and eat, not just cans and them left on the sand.

You are soothed and so you look up and around.

The drawl belongs to an older woman with henna-ed hair and a long beaded necklace. 'Such a 'mare,' she is saying as, hands latex-gloved, she shuffles the cakes behind the perspex counter. 'And just when we'd got all sorted for the season. Had to go straight away, she said. Now, and she pointed at herself and then at the sky. Fly today, I must fly today. Here—just hold this for a sec.' She passes a half-empty plate out to the girl at the till, rearranges the others to create the space at the back, takes the plate back and slots it in. 'I made out it was something to do with her mother,' she says, 'something funny going on, something wrong in the head as far as I could tell.' You hear the dull sound as she bats herself twice on the left ear for emphasis and as her arm comes up the beads that were caught round her breast swing freely towards the sticky-iced cakes. 'So she's back in Germany', she says, 'and we're left up the bloody creek.'

Then from the teenager by her side: 'She was alright, though, wasn't she? Completely fine to have around. I liked her. And super-shiny hair.' She is polishing forks, dipping them one by one into steaming water and rubbing them dry, letting them clatter into a plastic box.

'Shiny bloody hair, my foot,' her employer says, 'I've never had a German before and I never will again. My mother, she said, my mother, and something about a spa and "her head it is ill". So I let her go.'

You begin to listen with the first hint of a purpose.

'And the paper's no good at this time of year. Anyone any good is sorted by now. Any friends of yours not fixed up yet? No? Sod's law. It'll have to be the paper then, but I tell you I'm going to see a lot of duds.'

Without noticing it, you have smoothed down your own non-shiny hair, and retied it into its knot on your neck. You stand up.

'Are you, I mean, looking? For a waitress, I mean?'

The henna-ed woman unbends and looks at you, looks across at the girl who shrugs her little shoulders, looks at you again. Five minutes later you are officially employed for the next two months with a trial of a week.

'Call me Sandy,' she says, and she squeezes your hand and lets it go.

You ask Sandy where you can find a room. 'A room?' she asks. 'To stay in?'

'To stay in'.

'Oh,' she says, 'you really have just arrived. I thought—' But she remembers the paper and, worse, the church notice board and she bites her tongue against what it was that she thought. And so ten hours after you left your flat you are giving rent and your previous landlord's address as a reference to Sandy's sister Jan who has dark roots growing out, bony hips and a tiny back room in her B&B which is only five minutes away on the top of the cliff.

II

And to all appearances you have, as they say, fallen on your feet. It turns out you are perfectly good at the job. It requires the ability to perform a series of repetitive movements at a consistent level of energy and with a degree of manual dexterity. You can do that, and you do it better because it allows you no time to think. You too polish cutlery in boiling water, refill and empty the dishwasher, tip leftovers into the foot-pedal bin, remove sandwich debris from the plughole. You grow accustomed to the drawl and the patter through the swing door behind you and begin to paste Sandy and Jenny's names onto their conversations with customers and then into the chatter between themselves. They develop a place of their own in your expanded mind.

Time passes quickly. And though she does not say it, Sandy is happy enough. She does not know or need to know that your concentrated precision is the result of a near-crippling fear of being caught out. She does not know that your body is stretched to absorb a wave of adrenalin every time she opens the swing door. She only knows that her new kitchen girl is better than that German was and probably good enough to help out front. Quiet, though, she thinks, and so just before closing time she sends chattering Jenny in to lend you a hand and, door wedged open, listening, tidies the front herself.

All the washing up is done and you are drying off the last plates from the dishwasher while Jenny wipes down the stainless steel cabinets with baby oil. You are giving your task more concentration than it needs, suddenly self-conscious, wanting both to show you are doing your job and to ward off any need to talk. Jenny is oblivious.

'Busy out there today,' she says. 'Only just done with clearing and the next table sitting down. 'Cos it's cold outside—and anyway Saturday's always mad. You OK in here?' You nod. 'Cool. Yeah, always OK if the dishwasher's going right. Crazy day last week, it gave up and I was in here washing everything up and then the guy came to mend it, and I was like "'scuse me - I need to get past the door", and he was going "it'll be ready in a mo', move over darling I need to get at that switch behind the fridge". And he had five cups of tea I kept making for him and it took, like, forever. Cute guy. Making eyes at me but I said I'm taken. I could tell he wanted more, you know, you can always tell. Lucky you weren't here last week—I was OK but not what you need on your first day.'

'No,' you say. 'I get what you mean.' You are concentrating on wiping each last drop of water off the hot crockery and stacking it steadily on the shelves above the sink, but you are also looking surreptitiously at Jenny. (You are mesmerised by her confidence.) She is shorter than you except for her shoes, black patent with the high heels battered where they've gone down gaps in the pavement and creases cracking open across the toe. Her opaque tights are bobbled and her skirt pulled tight across them. In the heat of the café her eye make-up has gone blotchy with flakes of mascara on her cheeks, and her heavy foundation has slid down so you see her shiny skin. Reapplied hastily throughout the day, pink lip gloss still sings out of her face.

'So where're you from?' Jenny asks. 'Up North? Near Manchester? Cool. I've a mate up there at uni. She says the nightlife is totally awesome. Not like here,' and she rolls her eyes and rubs baby oil firmly into the gap between the hinges then swears as the screws catch and tear the cloth.

'And you're staying with Jan? Yeah, I know Jan. In here all the time; more like best friends than sisters. Like it?'

'Yes,' you say. 'It's fine. It's good'.

You have been taken aback by Jenny's invasion of what all day has felt like your space, but now you are relaxing again. You feel no threat.

'You know anyone down here?' Jenny asks.

And you say, 'No.'

'You'll meet people, though,' she says, without hesitation. 'The bars are rubbish but people still go. Usually at least some nice boys,' she says, and adds with a smile, 'not that I'm looking, of course'. She pauses and you notice and you know that some response is needed but you do not know what and so you nod and smile and then look down at the plate you're holding and rub at it particularly hard. 'What about you,' Jenny starts up again, 'anyone special?'

'Mmmmm,' you say, and your heart gets hot and you smile harder. Then as though something you've been holding back is seeping into your veins you say, 'Yeah. Yeah, sort of. I'm with a guy. Adam. No, he's not down here. Well not really going out with him, but, y'know, he's sort of special.' And what was merely seeping has flooded through your body and you are surprised and ashamed at what you have said and done.

Jenny is crouched down, polishing, her knees apart for balance, one ankle rolled awkwardly outwards so the scratched upper of her shoe is against the floor. She notices nothing. 'Go on then,' she says, without looking up, 'what's he like?'

You breathe deeply, and then you think to yourself, why not? Why is this not a story I can tell? And you say: 'Like? Well, sort of, I guess, sort of tall. He lives back north. His name's Adam.' And then more careful, with sudden trepidation at where this could go: 'I guess we're on a break, a bit of a break.'

(Sandy, listening the other side of the door, is reassured that you're not so much of a loner as she'd feared. Yes, she thinks, you'll be fine out front. She'll give you a few days and then she'll try you out.)

'Oh,' Jenny says, and her brow pulls in in automatic sympathy. 'It'll be OK – we all have breaks.' She has stopped polishing and is looking up to check you're not too upset. 'Damien dumped me last month but now we're totally together again. Look—he gave me this bracelet, said he was really sorry. And it's not like he cheated on you.' She holds out her wrist for admiration.

'No,' you say, 'no'. But there is a swelling just under your eyes which is an expression of guilt and in your mind a voice says 'jumped pretty quick into bed, didn't you?' and the bit you have added yourself: 'you slut, you whore'. You shake your head. 'Yeah, it'll be OK,' you say and hang up your tea-towel by the side of the sink.

'Anyway...' and you stand for a moment, wrists as though handcuffed behind you, back to the wall.

Then from the doorway Sandy says, 'OK, Rachel— that's it for you. You can head off now. Eight am tomorrow, love.'

'That's great,' you say, and 'bye,' you say, and, careful, wary of being like yesterday's bloody woman, you close the outside door behind you as you go.

You walk away down the sea front trying to breathe relaxation through the puppet feeling that has taken hold again of your limbs. You are pained to know they are now discussing you, Jenny leaning on the doorframe waiting for her guy and Sandy checking the day's takings on the side by the till. She's OK, your mind hears them say. Not that friendly; a bit quiet and odd. Weird she's come down here just like that. Must be more than a break. But she'll be OK. And then more positive (and you allow yourself a hesitant smile of pride): maybe she'll come out of herself a bit; seems nice enough. Let's wait and see.

The waves keep on breaking on your left. You continue to walk beside them. Then eventually you find that your mind has for some time been blank and with that you turn back again and up the steps up the cliff and towards your new home.

III

To start with that is how your days unfold: from eight till six you are absorbed by a constant low level of action and talk, then you spend your evenings alone in your room watching whatever is on the small TV. As your biographer I am proud that you can manage that. It is a step forward from where you have been. Your responsibilities are few, but you are honouring them. I am proud of you also as your friend. But you are looking up. That is not all; there is more, you say. Tell me, I say, even with increased pride; tell me how it is that you have grown.

You settle yourself comfortably in your chair. You sip at your red mug of tea. You begin.

It is a week later. It is evening. And today for the first time you are not tired out simply because you have to get up early and because your days are full. So though the café closes as usual at six, rather than going straight home you do what the tourists do who are flooding the town: you pause on the first unoccupied bench you come to and you look out to sea.

On the horizon a ship caught side-on by the westerly light glows like a neon message board. Closer in a buoy, orange like the disc of that sun, bobs irregularly on a tight diagonal, tethered against the swell of the waves. A man and woman are meandering along the shifting edge of the water, leaving their footprints in the sand. You follow their progression across your line of sight. They are slowed almost to awkwardness by each one's arms around the other's back. They are absorbed in this moment, are unconcerned that their footsteps are already softened, rounded, melting away. You watch. And muscle by muscle as you see them move you realise that you too are beginning to relax. Your shoulders unclench and your triceps loosen and your elbows release gently backwards to rest on the slats of the bench. Your abdomen, too, eases outwards. Your eyes are drawn to the edge of the beach and the relentless gentle scalloping swarm of the waves.

The breeze pulls your hair across your face.

The sound of the waves is airbrushed away.

You are relaxed and safe in this new place, you say, and you breathe right in and then out from your heart. You are content.

The couple, you see, have slowed to a halt, are turned inwards on each other, face to face, are cupping each other's cheeks, temples, hair. You are content, you say again. And you continue to watch. But as still they stand in that encircling embrace there is something that is ringing, something rising in your brain.

You need not tell me why: Adam is on your mind, I say. You look up and you blink. You are surprised, I tell you that I've guessed your trouble; but there is no surprise here. You disagree. It is, you say, not that you are remembering him. (He is holding her hair back, pulling it down at the nape of her neck so gently her face tips to meet his lips.) No, you say, it is that the memory of him and the pain it awakens are just now oddly sharp. 'Oddly sharp,' I repeat to you. Oddly? Really? (A flush wakes up your pulse and you will it down and away.) Listen: it is clear what you're hiding from. Continue to watch this man and this woman here, and remember what it is that you have done. You have deserted a sensitive and a struggling man, a man to whom you brought a lifeline of hope, one to whom you had offered your virgin love. You led him on, I tell you, and then without warning you left him.

You start to disagree again. (You know that he corrupted you.) But then you stop. You wait a moment. (Your body is once again calm.) You admit that despite your relaxed enjoyment of the sight of the ship, the buoy, the couple, the waves, that just now Adam takes up more of your brain than he has ever done before. For a moment you are disconcerted by that thought, and you swallow hard and you blink. But then you think back to Sandy and Jenny and the café and your new life, and you feel quietly secure. You decide to allow your thoughts to emerge, but with tight precision, as though you are piping icing.

You are, you admit to me, feeling some guilt. Your farewell was a little abrupt; you didn't allow him to get used to the idea; you barely got used to the idea yourself. Looking back now you do not know what it was that so suddenly made you feel that way. (It was the sunlight on rough bricks, the smell of food, an anemone unfurling with the tide.)

But then you are stronger. Why, you say, should you feel guilt when there was so little tenderness there? You remember Richard's confidence in your intimacy and how there was no link between that and what you felt. You remember Adam's loss of all adult control. That he refused to take the pan off the hot hob. That he was feeling at you like a child with its mother. (As though its mother will in a moment be forever gone.)

You say (as though this is conclusive) that, yes, you went to bed with him. But that you did not bleed.

Then you pause. You want to shelve him, to move on, to get on with your life. But your chest tightens with a discomfort you cannot rationalise away. You need, you say again, to move on. (You are concentrating on looking out to sea.) Tears appear in the corners of each eye and tip over and down your face. You absorb them with the end of your sleeve, pulling it down and over your thumb and dabbing at your cheeks carefully, as though you were wearing make-up.

You look out to sea and you dab at your face. And as you do a gentleman in a lightweight mackintosh sits down beside you—then instantly, with an apology, he stands up again, and you say, 'no, don't be sorry,' and you sniff and you gulp, and he says again, 'I'm sorry,' and you wonder how he can know what it is he is so certainly sorry for, and slowly he sits down again at your side. And then there are two of you. (Three, we might say.) He is close enough to be in your field of vision and now he is here you do not wish to confuse him by moving away. So you do what is easier for you; and for a time you continue to sit, and now you watch the beach, its debris, the waves, and half of a tailored arm. (Your tears stop of their own accord.)

'Do you need a walk?' he asks.

'Maybe,' you say. You pause, you wait for him to go away. You breathe more shallowly, not wanting him to hear you, suddenly conscious he might see the shell of your body move. (And with relief: Adam did not see you when you worshipped the dawn.) The waves slop and they slop at the dirtying sand. And then, into his silence, guilty that you are refusing this man's offered help, you say, 'Yes, I should go for a walk.'

He stands up, and he bends his right arm and holds it out, stiff, ready for you to take. 'A walk,' he says, and you do not say, 'I didn't mean, there's no need, no, not at all'. Instead you stand too and you take his arm.

Then it is simple; you walk back along the sea front towards town, past the arcades and the shops and the pillar box which have all been there for a century or more, and you go onto the pier and then you turn and you walk back again. He moves precisely, tidily, always firmly forward as though he knows that alone you would stumble; he is like a father guiding a child. You take courage from the continued pressure of his arm. You are comfortable at his side. You breathe more deeply and your bobbing heart slows down. You start merely to be sure that your blood is being pumped round your body.

And despite his proximity nothing about his presence obtrudes into your life. He is, you think, dapper despite his grey hair, despite his age, and you feel that term, 'dapper', blow out on your lips, but then it floats harmlessly away. You walk to the end of the pier and then back and when you return he reaches your bench and lets go your arm. 'Look,' he says, and he points to the brass plaque screwed onto the blue back of the bench. He reads it out: '" For those who perish on the sea". That, at least, we do not face.'

Then he thanks you for your company, and with middle-aged dignity he takes his leave. He crosses the road, leaves your café on his right and turns the corner by the charity shop. That night you lie in bed and you smile, and you do not cry. It is as though that walk has introduced a balance to your life. His arm was a comfort to you and it does not matter that you do not know his name.

IV

The effect of that comfort is lasting. When you wake up
the next morning you are more calm and breathing more
deeply, engaging and swelling the full width of your chest
as well as the hard bump of your diaphragm. Each breath
pushes down into the crevices of your body like pastry
pressed into a pie dish. Out of bed, your feet are firmer
on the floor: you feel your toes relaxing to spread out into
the carpet, feel the plump outer curve of each foot and
the point where the instep leaves and then returns to the
ground. As you stand you can rock from one side to the
other and then forwards and back, and as you do you
feel heavier, more grounded, as though there is a valued
connection between you and the world.

You look different, too. Your jaw is softer, your eyes
wider open, your smile more real. As you walk to work
people smile in turn at you, and, though subconsciously,
you notice that, and so you arrive and push open the door
with a lightness that is new to you.

Sandy looks up at the burst of air, and, 'Oh,' she says,
deflated, 'I was hoping you were Jenny.'

'She's not here yet?' you ask, and inside you swells a
bubble of sweet, almost proprietorial, pride.

'No,' with a firm shake of the henna-ed head.

'I didn't see her,' you say, and then the bubble bursts and
you wonder why you feel that is your fault.

'Damn,' says Sandy. 'She should've been here an hour
ago.' Then, 'Look; the place's almost empty; there's some
stuff I really need to get done—' and she hesitates again
and then she sees your cheeks still brightened by your

walk, your hair blown soft by the wind, and she says with greater confidence, 'Let me show you how it all works out front. You might as well do some serving if Jenny's going to be late. I'll stick around out here to keep an eye. It'll do her good to do the kitchen for a while.'

And so it is mid-morning and you are out front. There is still an uncertainty in the air, as though in Jenny's absence you have lost the buffer that protected you against the direct feel of the world. But you have learned how to make all the coffees, know never to lift the arm out of the milk while it's frothing, know how the till works and how to count out change. The place is ticking over but not full-on and you are getting more efficient, relaxing into your work. ('You learn fast', you have been told, though you did not believe it enough to hear.) Nonetheless, Sandy is seated at a table near-by, listening to you as she works through a stack of papers. She is making slow biro notes in the margins of each sheet. Her letters are rounded like beach pebbles.

Just after eleven the door pushes more heavily open and Jenny pours in out of the wind and heads directly for the counter. Sandy looks up from her paperwork, gestures hard towards the kitchen and follows her through the swing door.

You are at the till: 'That's two-fifty, three, five and ten,' you say and you place the heavy teapot down. You watch the customer step away from the counter, balancing her flexing tray against the weight of the handbag cutting into her arm. Imperceptibly but automatically your shoulders have gone up in sympathy, with the customer or with Jenny (you do not know which), have hardened against a coming blow, and your breath is already more shallow. You are attuned to a different force in the air, afraid at the disruption of the attained status quo. (Jenny would say that the vibes are wrong.) Then, 'God, girl,' you hear Sandy's stage-whisper. 'What the hell do you think you're doing? Three bloody hours late you are. What if it'd been busy, and with Rachel so new?' and your body settles automatically into a rigidity which this morning you would have thought you had left behind.

Customers continue to need to be served. You serve them. But you have become more precise in the way you hold the cake slice, in the way you place the cup centrally to catch the boiling stream of espresso. You speak more loudly as though to hide a wash of shame.

Then Sandy puts her head round the door and gestures you towards her. 'Here a sec', she says, and her brusque energy repels you so your feet are slow to move. You expect to see her frown, you see in your mind the shadow of a raised arm (in Jenny's place this is what you know you'd deserve, what you'd expect from Sandy's hard impatience, from the voice that dismissed so harshly the German girl's pain and which hired you so decisively instead); but the frown is not there. Instead you see that her face is soft. 'Crying her heart out, poor lamb', she says, and she looks around the room. 'You alright here?' she asks, and then, 'Thank God it's pretty quiet.'

It is more than pretty quiet. Currently there is nothing for you to do: the counter clear, the machines wiped clean of coffee grounds and bubbled, slopped milk. So you are standing a foot back from the till, your back to the kitchen wall, your ears attuned to Jenny's muffled voice.

'It's like she doesn't care for me anymore,' she wails. 'Like he's the only one. She's like, don't be so jealous now, Jennifer, don't be a child, and she's standing there looking at herself in the mirror, says she needs to live her life and it's not fair for me to stop her but she's just not there anymore.' The meaning is clear but you have to concentrate to catch the words; around you the customers are doing the same. No-one catches anyone else's eye. 'It's like she's dumped me now she's got him.' Then a long drawn-in stuttering breath and a reply from Sandy, quiet, something you cannot hear. 'Yes-s-s-s', you hear, and then again, more quietly, 'yes-s-s;, it's just so hard, not me and her anymore.' 'Shush, honey', you now hear Sandy's deeper voice, and as though she has decided to be more firm, 'shush, now, quietly, my love,' and for a moment both the kitchen and the tables are silent. Then a noisy family enters in a rush and the silence is broken; you can no longer hear and nor can the customers and so they start again with relief to talk and you are bending to get drinks out of the fridge and making a tea with lemon and ignoring as the mother does the children's calls for cake. Slowly you relax again. Then Sandy comes out and takes over the till.

You go round the tables, clearing and wiping them for a little longer than you need to, stacking the plates and cups onto a tray. With their weight on your forearms you edge your hip into the kitchen tentatively, your body following as unobtrusively as you can make it. But your caution is wrong, because inside it is as though nothing has happened. 'Hi,' says Jenny, and from behind your tray you smile carefully towards her. 'Yep, fine,' she says, as though you had asked. 'Row with my mum; that man of hers. Yeah, sorry. PMT as well. You OK out front?'

'Fine,' you say, and then you pause, confused by the rapid disappearance of a state which to you would have been momentous. Your arms load the dirties into the dishwasher. Your face is down. But Jenny is unembarrassed. 'Sandy was cool with it,' she says, 'like she was my mum.' Disconcerted, she sniffs, then sniffs again and tosses her head. As she talks she is rummaging two-handed through her handbag like a keen puppy digging in the sand. She pulls out and peers into a folding mirror. 'God, just look at me,' she says, and she spits on a tissue, rubs it round her eyes, then, holding the mirror in her left hand, relines her eyelids, smudges the liner roughly into her still-red skin and, mouth open like a cartoon goldfish, applies her mascara. 'I look terrible,' she says, and you say, 'No, no you don't; you look fine.'

Jenny ignores you: 'Damien's gonna think I've gone mad or something,' she says, 'I've texted him to come and get me. Sandy said I should, said it was quiet enough, that I should get him to come and give me a hug.' And with the mention of Damien she tries out a smile to herself, careful in the tiny mirror. She finds a tube of ice-pink gloss and smooths it on. You are awkward.

'Really, you look fine,' you say, and Jenny looks blankly through you, as though it is nothing you could understand.

'Anyway,' she says, and she is superior to you once again; her need for care is over; there is nothing you can do.

It is when he arrives that you realise why. He comes right through into the kitchen to find her. You are there as she snuggles into his chest, as she balls up his sweatshirt in her fists, as his arms go round her as stiff protection despite his A-frame stance and his embarrassed stare. You cannot help watching though you know you should turn away. You see Jenny stay in his arms though now her eyes are long-dry. You exchange a glance and a shy smile with Damien. And though you think that you are separate and afraid finally something relaxes in your mind.

(I too pause and I smile for you. I smile as though a spectator at God's Creation.

But you look up. I have disturbed your train of thought you say. You have not finished. So, continue.)

You continue. And what you say is that you are realising

that you feel both excited and afraid. This is why:

Jenny and Sandy are showing you a different way of life. Everything that you have read or heard has told you that humanity reaching out to humanity is the way of the world. That from parent to child, from lover to beloved, there is a phenomenon known as unconditional love. That disagreement and anger, that declaration of what you think, feel, prefer can go hand in hand with continued attachment. You have read all of this and you have not believed it. You have known it to be a fiction. For that reason it has never surprised you that you have not felt it. But you have watched Jenny and Sandy disagree and then heard them laugh together again. You have heard that Jenny and Damien have had a break, yet have seen each part of the other despite it all. What you have realised is that other people have something strong within them. (For now let us term it emotional security.) That for them relationships are not about protecting your self as one apart. You have realised this. And you are taking the next step: you are wondering whether it can be this way for you.

Let us be clear, your bravery here is immense. What you are considering is allowing someone else responsibility for maintaining even the smallest element of the sanity that you have fought for so hard. But this, you realise with a leap of your heart, is what you yearn to share. So when Jenny suddenly looks up, sees you watching, smiles and invites you out that evening with her mates (clubbing, Hotshots on Green Street, nine o'clock—it's a bar as well as a club) you take a deep breath and you say, 'Yes, please.' Here's my number, she says, just in case.

You know that you are honoured.

(You swallow down the rising of that honour in your throat.)

V

You arrive, you say, deliberately late. Half an hour ago you nearly sent a text to say you couldn't come, that you had got food-poisoning, or a migraine, or you just weren't well. But your head reeled through how it would be tomorrow morning as you see Jenny did not believe you, as you blush and stutter, as she tells Sandy you lied and did not show up. And so out of fear you make yourself go. Ready and fidgeting for an hour beforehand, you set off late and then take the least direct route you can, approaching the club in ever-decreasing circles until unavoidably you are outside its doors. They are papered over with posters which have peeled and peeled away in the salty air until you see the black-painted metal underneath. Above them, unobscured, 'Hotshots' stands out in stiff silver letters edged in lights.

Though it is barely dark there is a queue outside. You join it. You are the only person not with friends. (You try to look unconcerned; you look around with a vague smile; you feel that your heart is beating fast.) You avoid meeting the bouncer's eyes. (You know that you should not be here.) But with his fat hand he gestures you through beyond the ropes and in a strip-lit corridor you hand over ten pounds to the dreadlocked girl in the kiosk.

You walk as instructed through the swing-door, and sound which until now has been muffled slams into you. You stop; you take a step back and to the side. It is dark, but a darkness cut through with sudden sheets of light. Flashes sear your retinas and then the whole world disappears. There are only instantaneous shapes, then nothing. You blink, and blink, and fake smoke rises in front of you so the people you see are jerky floating torsos, and then again they are gone.

You stand, and take two deep breaths, and tell yourself that you are in a night-club, that is all. You notice that the music has no words. You see that there is purple and blue in the light. You swallow down the expectation that you will be stood up. You remember you are honoured to be here.

But you cannot see Jenny in the loose-knit, clustering crowd. You walk round the outside of the room looking unconcerned, wanting no-one to see you, stepping always to the side to wait as people edge past with swaying handfuls of drinks. And after a while your head begins to accept the constantly reaffirmed darkness, the mechanical movements of the dancers, the music, the smoke, the crowd. With each flash you scan the faces closest by, then squeeze politely, unnoticed, on to the next group. But it does not after all take you long; Jenny (you look closely, you check that it is her), Jenny is wearing a shiny animal print bomber jacket over a tight mini-dress and heels so high that even this early on she is leaning on Damien for support. He is in dark jeans and a paler tee-shirt, with a chain belt loose against his skinny thighs. When you arrive she is hanging ostentatiously on his arm discussing loudly with herself whether to stick her new jacket in the cloakroom. 'Nah, fuck it,' you hear as you sidle up. 'Stuff always gets stolen. And look at the fucking queue.' She shakes her head so her hair swings forward over her eyes and then tosses it back. It glides across the satin of the jacket and in the instant of light you see it twitch with static.

You stand there. Unnoticed. Then, 'Hi, there, hello,' you say; and, louder, 'Jenny—hi, it's Rachel,' and you force yourself to tap on her padded shoulder. She looks round with the frown of irritated non-recognition that you expect. Then she smiles. (Your heart smiles in response.)

'Hey there,' she says. 'You made it. Thought you wouldn't come.' And then: 'Baz, Sam, Mick—hey, guys, this is Rach.' Two boys and a girl turn briefly to face you and peer to see who you are. 'Rach,' she emphasises again. 'From work.' You smile. You nod. You, too, say, 'Hey.'

Then you stand there at their shoulders and watch as the girls carry on their conversation. They shout through cupped hands into each other's ears. You try to look interested. You laugh when they do. Your face, you feel, is stiff. Sam, you see, is with Mick ('it's Michelle,' she bawls; she is next to you, she's the one you can hear), and the two are draped across each other in nonchalant angles in a mirror image of Damien and Jenny. In the constantly re-forming smoke and darkness the two couples appear doubled. They are gesturing and shouting and laughing and you do not know how they can hear what they say. In a pause you say you'll go to the bar. No-one hears you. No-one replies.

When you come back they have all gone off to dance. (Part of you feels relief.) You rest six perspiring throw-away glasses of vodka and coke on the chest-height shelf that runs round the wall, then ease yourself onto a sticky bar stool. You pull your feet in and onto the foot-rest, retract them carefully away from anyone passing by. And then you watch the group of friends as they dance. Jenny is at their centre. She is a mime of laughter, of extravagance, of youthful play. The others circle round her, less confident, but moving all in time all the same. They, too, are miming unthinking fun with their bodies, though their faces are studiedly blank. You watch from the darkness of the side of the room, and as you watch a sickness turns over in your chest.

(You are pummelled by the flashing lights and the noise. Without noticing it you are retreating from who you are. From who you are learning to be.)

You take one of the tumblers and drink it down. You rub your hand across your mouth. You cough.

You turn away from these people whom you hardly know and towards the centre of the dance-floor. (Immediately you feel that you are safely alone.) Your eyes hook onto a couple whose dancing has a shape as though they are in control, as though they are not merely jerking with triggered reflex nerves. The girl is taking her prominence seriously. She is poised, precise, technically good, locking her eyes on her partner's face as her body pirouettes, then flicking her head instantly round at the end of each spin. She is in tight jeans and a loose, silver, low-cut top, her sweat-curled hair bundled high on her crown. (You think that you have never seen such glamour.) Her partner is a less good dancer and also more drunk. He reels her in and pushes her out again with growing inaccuracy and she is progressively knocked off balance until even from a distance her smile is forced. After a while they stop and he goes to the bar. She stands to the side, alone, puffing a little, looking around at the other dancers and into the middle-distance, challenging anyone else to approach. She, too, has a presence which awakens in you a pain. (Her smile, perhaps. Or the separateness of her gaze.) You look down. You drink your vodka fast. Then you let your eyes lose their focus and the dancers become a mere moving mass, and you something held apart. The noise and momentarily solid slants of light become a protection against their demands, make you invisible to the bumping, affectionate world around you. Without trying you fall into habit: you lock your thoughts out of your brain, you replace them with the mesmeric beat (you do not feel its happiness; it is a world apart from where you are).

Time, you find, is stationary. Repeatedly you look at your watch, concentrating hard to read numbers which never move on. (This evening will have no end.) You focus your eyes on a point on the floor, concentrate on allowing no distraction until you no longer feel it when people bang into you as they pass. (You are ugly, you think, but you are not really here.) But for all that you try to pull yourself away your head inhabits a growing sense of movement; is being propelled through a tunnel at increasing pace. You try to slow it down. You force yourself to look around.

You see that the wall beside you is mirrored, is pushing your still reflection back. You blink at your second self and it disappears for an instant. Then it is there again; a solemn face with hair pulled tight back. There is no spark, no life as it sits in the shiny wall. It floats, pale, above your black polo-neck. You put out a hand to push it away, and feel the cold, smooth surface. You pull back your hand, rub it warm. What you feel is a rush of hatred and shame that they are dancing and that this is what you are. You look away from your face. And then back. Again it disappears as you blink, but then, watching closely, you see its eyes move.

You are suspended, timeless, in a tunnel of light and noise; you let your mind slip away.

From your distant outpost you see Jenny swaying back from the dance-floor, sweating in the colourless flashing lights and laughing, pulling on Baz's arm. You do not move. (You do not know why.) You wait for her approach. And then, 'Here,' you say, 'I got you a drink,' and you hand over the one remaining, now-warm tumbler. She looks confused. Then, 'OK, cool,' she says. 'How're you doing?' You say that you are OK, that you are fine. 'Yeah,' you say, 'having a good time.' Your words feel elongated in your mouth and as though they are coming out at the wrong pitch. Your lips are rubbery. Your throat contracts and you hear a sharp, high laugh.

'Hey, come and dance,' Jenny says. 'Dance with Baz,' and she pulls at him and he turns and looks at you as though he can no longer remember who you are.

'Go on,' she says, and so you say 'OK,' and you allow yourself to follow the space he creates back across the floor, and then you start to dance with Baz.

To start with you keep yourself cut off. You half-feel his hands on the outside of your body. You hold yourself a little gap away. Your gaze goes over his shoulder, eyes unfocussed, a constant half smile on your face. But then you begin to relax and then to feel a growing pleasure. It is, you say in retrospect, the music. Its beat, you say, is taking you over. It is enacting some kind of sorcery. (You look around. You see it in everyone's eyes.) People are jumping up and down with increasing energy. They are pulled by the music, forced to hold its beat. Blank faces soften into laughter in the moments of light.

You, too, begin to move without self-conscious thought, letting your hips angle themselves forward so that you are groin to groin and you link your hands on Baz's damp back. The two of you swing from side to side, in time, in time, in time, and then—as your weight goes out a handsbreadth too far—with a jolt and a stumble and a tightened grip. His grip and not yours. For you, laughing, are pulling and swaying away, turning your back to him, placing his hands on your hip bones, holding them with your hands in place. (You think that the placing is nonchalant, is cool. I tell you it has the sophistication of flaccid flat-fish slapped down on a fishmonger's counter. This man, I say, is not for you.) Your four knees bend in shared zigzags. The world is warm around you. You feel glamorous, as though you too are wearing silver lurex. You stop noticing the stickiness of the floor and the crunch of broken glass. You close your eyes. You are happy to dance.

Time that was so slow now hurtles unnoticed on.

Later you retreat from the dance-floor and onto a sofa in the corner which is supposed to be leather and which is wet with drinks. Vaguely you hear the others' voices. Now they are louder than the music, though you still cannot hear what they say. You are sitting tipped sideways, half on Baz's knee and half on the sofa, squashed up against Michelle. Your elbows are on the low table, and your head is in your hands. 'Fine,' you say, 'just fine,' whenever anyone asks. Your voice emerges with a high-pitched laugh, but you are sure, you are really very sure—if anyone asks, your head says, and it is distorted like a radio station going out of range, you are sure that that is good.

But at some point you find your head begins to ache. You are tired of straining to hear and your throat is sore with shouting. You start to compose in your swinging head non-sequential fragments of a speech about how you need to get home, get some sleep. You assemble it, ready. Then next to you someone vomits on the floor and it splashes up onto Damien's trousers. And he jumps up, and 'Shit!' he says, 'Fuck, fuck it that's gross!' and while they are all shouting and swaying and deciding whether to leave you find that you have said goodbye, said that you've got to go, and without noticing how slow and uncertain you are you have felt your way out to the main door, have smiled like a cherub at the tattooed bouncer, are in the cold street.

You do not remember how you get home. But when you get there you switch on the ceiling light and lie down, feel the room swirl around, put a foot out to stop it. Your ears are muffled as though they hold a constant sound of the sea. You take off your shoes and lift them to your face and closely you inspect one and then the other. Each has tiny diamonds embedded in the sole. You smile at the diamonds and tap the soles against each other so they make a scratchy clink. Then, still clothed, still smiling, you lie back and then you fall asleep.

VI

You are there, unmoving, unconscious, defenceless. And there for the moment you will stay. Here I take over. No alternative offered.

You are, I say, disgracefully drunk. You have danced, you have flirted with—been petted by—this youth. Greasy. Pimpled. Thin-limbed. Also drunk. He has no dignity, I tell you with energy. He desecrates our tale.

Yes, you say, you danced, and you are defiant. You say that you had a good time. You say that you have waited too long to be allowed such simple fun. You say that I'm obliged to include this now: that Jenny is your friend and Baz is too; that, pimpled or not, he made you laugh.

You threw yourself at him, I counter.

And you say, no. You simply did what it is that teenagers do. You did less, you say, than you did with Adam. And I condoned that, you add under your breath.

I pause. I am taken aback. That was, I tell you, not the same.

But if you insist then we can start from there. For I grant you that Adam was not all we hoped. That he was finally not your appointed fate. And I grant you that Baz is not Adam. I give you that, but that is all. (I have a casting role in this tale and Baz will not be the male lead.)

You say you don't care, and that this is not my story but your life. You danced with Baz. B-A-Z.

And, O my love, (my tears rise and behind my voice is a sob): do you value our friendship so little, I ask. Do you forget what we have done? Think back, I say; remember our journey; remember all we have suffered together; remember your panic and how I helped you breathe; remember how we have been as one. (You look across at me with alarm. I see it. I sob more loudly.) Then (you are watching): my dear, I can give you so much more than this. It does not have to be this way. You have met a man, I say, who is worthy of you (and worthy also of me). That is where your tale should turn.

You look perplexed. You grip at my hand. Your hand shakes despite its grip. I ask you to follow me here.

Listen. (I dry my tears on a lace-edged if dirty handkerchief. I smile.) I understand the steps you have made into the world. Their difficulty. Your bravery. Your fight. I am with you as I always have been. So trust me now. Let me now take on the tale, let me carry it on to the next stage: this (not through Baz) is how you come to believe in love.

VII

It is mid-July and the town is sardine-full: of sticky-oily-skinned tourists, of rowdy exchange students, of retirees with walking sticks eking out their lives in the stinging mist that rises from the waves, of drunken-grouped survivors of summer exams. Late-night dog walkers harvest squeals from the beach as they disturb teenagers whose fumblings are excited by the novel solidity of the smell of the sea and the insidious roughness of the sand.

That busyness is appropriate to how you are. You have not only settled into feeling at home here, but have by default also allowed that home to be peopled. Both Sandy and Jenny have learned that you can give their chatter at least a partial response, and so you are becoming part-linked to them. You are allowing the scene a human narrative: those who approach you you are permitting to stay.

Take mascara-ed Jenny and A-frame Damien. I am content for their embarrassed affection to form for you the ideal of young love. (Neither directly threatens your purity, we agree.) Next to them, Sandy, childless, over-brusque, is nonetheless the central figure of maternity; she has placed her guard over the three of you, and is indulging you at the end of every day with the cakes that go off in the heat. Jan, more bony, less maternal, (more 'aunt') says 'hi there' every morning and every night, and you know she would worry if you did not appear. (And your mackintosh-ed gentleman? Yes, in a moment we will talk too of him.)

You know that you are straying into a different world, that you are becoming a part of the loose weave of others' emotion around you. At first you were catching at its edges, half-blind, but then as the simple responses come back you have found an allowance of excitement; with the discovery of their simple emotions you start to look for their equivalent in yourself. You are beginning to ease out of near-silence and to find your own voice. In response to all of that your behaviour is beginning to change. When the café is quiet now you come out front to listen to the meaningless chat. Tentative, but present. Your default which for so long has been 'away' is now becoming 'towards'.

Yes, yes, you say, and I see the excitement rise in your face.

This is releasing a deeper source of value within you. Slow but sure. Let us take today for a sign of a change in the pattern. Morning. Tell me.

Morning? you ask, and an impatient frown crosses your face. (I know you do not quite yet see me again as kind.) Morning, early morning, I encourage you. I remember that it is not your best time. (You have told me this in confidence before.) I know that despite your productive day-time activities more than half of your life still happens (let us say it quietly) to the shadowy figures who haunt the edge of the night, whose faces are blood-drained, whose feet move, weighty, through knee-height swirling fog. I know these folk steal to and fro in your mind. (I can help you to remember them. This, when I sleep, is also what I know. We still have this in common, dear. I can still help you through.) Whether you see them or not they come. But let us not stray into their path now, my dear. Look back towards me, take my hand, grip it tightly. Yes, that's right. We just need that acknowledgement that despite all that you have learned and all that with difficulty you do you do still need me.

Hang on to my hand. I do not wish to keep you here, to hold your head below the surface of the daytime world. But you must acknowledge as you think of this that despite all that has changed you still need my help.

For it is as a result of this that still every morning you fight against emergence into the day. It is true that you are pulled towards wakefulness by light through the curtains and the first sounds of traffic and gulls. But that is where your normality stops. You cannot choose to hear the gulls as gentle and to see the pale sun. Instead your brain awakens charged with the new day to assume a greater fear. Sirens screech and instinctively you lock down against the world. Your eyes hold themselves tight closed and you focus on what you know cannot harm you too much. And so behind your eyelids soft-edged bleeding figures continue to come and go against a background of night. With their familiarity a degree of pain is normal to you. Your ability to bear it reliably holds you safe in the gap between the night and the day. That is how it always is; you lie, half-awake, and in fear you watch, and so, unknowing, you create a long-as-possible pause intended to negate the day.

But this morning something has changed. This is inexplicable but true. Let us take it on: today with the dawn you wake suddenly and fully and without fear. Today you wake with a light bright space in your mind. You acknowledge it with surprise. You watch it. The space does not fall away. Instead as you hold it in your mind (as you begin to believe in it), it swells and becomes—you do not need to think what it is—an unforeseen yearning to see the great wide sea pulsating in the pale morning light. And, still inexplicable, that yearning is so strong that without thinking you creep child-like through the house, unlock, pass through and lock the front door with a flick of your wrist on the dull gold key. (As though far back there was a time before your known mind's heaviness.) Out in the street you hesitate. But then the breeze reaches out a hand to your face and the weight is gone again out through the soles of your feet, and then your breath is unrestrained as you trip into a run down the cliff path, and out and along the waterfront.

Feel it, my darling. Let us feel it together. There is a lightness here which is new to you. I know as little as you where it comes from. But this is joy that your running feet feel as their delicate cages of bones and muscles compress and bounce back on the pale, dry tarmac, and your mouth is tipping upwards and opening until you are laughing, catching yourself with a smile, and then laughing again until your eyes are wet and the great sea blurs into the refraction of a single dream-giant diamond.

You blink and you blink as miniature rainbows come and go and again you feel the breeze on your face and your hands flap loose by your side. Light pours out of the tips of your fingers whose sudden sensitivity to the movement of your pulse draws a shiver that runs comprehensively up your arms and out through your body.

You stop running and you pant and you look at the brimming sea. You feel its oscillation as it cloaks the spinning world. Like a gazelle you turn your head from side to side, astonished at the beauty of daylight on water, and with the movement your brain further loosens its grip on your darkness. Life courses through you. It takes its place within you. You embrace, arms out, its innocence. And then caught in that flow you have a sudden belief: 'this is the glory of reality.' And nothing happens. Nothing stops it. Nothing in your brain clamps down against that simple expression; and so it attaches itself to your breath and for a moment you feel it moving smoothly, cool, in and out of your bellows ribs. The glory.

The glory.

You stand, arms out, pores open to absorb the day. You thirst to absorb its beauty. A tremor runs through you from head to toe.

And then as your movement stops what you had expected to happen happens. You are forsaken. Your heart contracts like a purpled fist. The muscles in your neck set like cement. And with that rigidity you are suddenly unfit. You need to heave to find your shallow breath. Your feet are merely heavy on the ground. Something dark spreads in the back of your mind, in the bulge above the stem of your neck, and you stop, and you rein yourself in. You breathe a controlled breath and you settle your shoulders down. You are surprised at yourself. Shame rises automatically and floods through your body. You shake out your cold hands, wipe them across your smeary eyes and push your hair back behind your ears.

(You acknowledge that you need me here.)

You smile at yourself again; a hard twist up of the corners of your mouth that you intend to look wry to anyone who is watching. (No-one is.) Then you set out at a briskish, purposeful pace back towards Jan's. You will, you think, tell her you needed a stroll to clear your head. A bit too much to drink last night, you will say. (And—in a whisper—such a beautiful, a glorious day.)

Neither Jan nor Sandy notices a change in you. But Jenny, younger, sees your face and asks, 'You liked Baz, then?' and you colour, and, 'What? Baz? Yeah he was OK,' you say. You continue to plate up the cakes. You are embarrassed. You are glad to seem off-hand. You move onto wrapping pairs of forks and spoons in red serviettes.

You are efficient, neat, conscientious. Then, 'God, no, not Baz,' you say to yourself, and your laugh, you tell yourself, tinkles, and something delicate runs down your arms and into your finger tips and you see the sea and you feel the contrasting rough paper against the cold, smooth metal.

It is in that instant that, turning to start making the sandwiches, you know that you are hooked like Velcro; you know that you are in love. The realisation in your mind is momentous. You catch your breath in its honour, and for a moment the light on the sea just glimmers on the early morning town. But then your joy lets it go in a rush and the whole world lights up. The glory, your mind is whispering, and the glory your pulse replies.

And that is all of it. You are changed by the glorious light. Your fingers become tender and precise. You slice open the warm baguettes, tuck lettuce leaves gently into their yeasty hinge, position ready-cooked crisp bacon in parallel lines, ease in firm slices of tomato.

You are buoyed aloft.

Time doubles its pace around you.

VIII

All the time you are thinking, imagining, wondering how you will tell him your love. So it is no surprise to you when, late on Friday afternoon, he pushes open the café door. (Your soul has, we could say, called to him and—yes!—he has come.)

There is, of course, a banal, a necessary positioning:

He is, he says, surprised to see you here. Didn't know you worked here. Goodness, well there we are! Though only today he was remembering you, recalling your walk together from the bench outside, and before that (though he does not say this to you) a girl on the front in an emerald scarf. That was, he says, why he came in here. Here and not anywhere else. Right opposite where he left you last time. Then he laughs; he says he might as well still have a drink. And so you serve him: a pot of breakfast tea and a slice of Bakewell tart. You say, with a smile, that you enjoyed your walk on the prom the other day. He offers you another walk if it would help. You expected this. You have no qualms about saying yes. (And he sees that you are happier than you were before.)

So when your shift finishes at six he drinks down the dregs of his tea and you leave together. You take what with this becomes your usual route, and when you return to the bench you suggest that you sit there together for a while. (He hesitates, and then he says 'Yes.')

You sit, and you contemplate your love. You know you need not ask what is in his mind. The strength of your feeling tells you it is shared. Lust, you know now, with some pride, is different. It is a hot or a cold thread running up and down within your torso, expanding and contracting muscles as it goes. (You remember Baz's hands on your hip bones, and then you push the memory away.) What you are feeling now, you tell me, and your look is shy (feminine modesty has come to you at last), this is a more encompassing warmth. It starts in your chest and radiates out to the tips of your fingers. It opens your eyes wider and relaxes the muscles in your neck. And when you hold hands (you are almost holding hands) it is transmitted also to him and there need be nothing to say.

You continue to sit there. You hear the gulls as they squawk and call. You hear the splash and the pull of the waves on the beach.

You sit there until the evening begins to cool, then you find you have agreed to go for dinner, and he stands up and you take his arm and you cross the road, walk along for a bit and step into a noisy bistro. Both of you order the menu du jour (onion soup, steak and chips, crème brulée), and he orders red wine and you drink it together. Then he is mostly the one who talks.

You remember something of what he says. That he is a civil servant, in Westminster, in London, with a fine view from his office of Big Ben and of Westminster Bridge. That that is where he finds himself during the week. But that he's taken to spending the weekends down here for the space and the quiet. That he is glad, so glad, that this weekend he is here. That he was coming here again looking for peace. That his mind is so full of a certain young girl. That she…but—no—let's not talk about that. That you are so young, so beautiful, so much like the picture that rises in his head. He confides that he saw you before that walk; that he saw you in your scarf, standing, looking out to sea, and his heart was drawn to you, and he waited and he watched until you were gone. That finding you in the café today made his heart leap. That he half-saw your profile, and then he was sure, and his pulse beat hard in his suddenly clammy hands. He talks, and you drink the wine he continues to pour, and you sit and you absorb all that he says. (You are memorising what you will say to Jenny tomorrow. You are planning that you will always now wear your scarf.)

He talks through the tough steak and through to dessert; but then over coffee his tone changes. He says that he shouldn't bother you with all of this. Says that it is good of you to listen to an old man. You say nothing. You do not wish to break the spell.

But anyway it is broken; for then he insists on paying and because, he says, it is late and the evenings can be rowdy he walks you all the way home. You remember that on his arm you are floating through the streets. That at your door he steps back, smiles, and says,

'Goodnight.'

You close the door behind him. You stand behind it and feel him walk away. You tiptoe, tripping, up the stairs, past Jan's closed door, into your tiny back room. You drop your weight onto your bed like a child. You hug yourself tight. Gravity eases your heels out of your shoes, the stiff leather wobbles from the ends of your toes and then tips off. You look up towards the dark ceiling and steady yourself with a foot which goes down on top of a shoe.

You smile.

You are relaxed into happiness. You continue to smile; and though momentary that continuity is enough to let past a thought that has a definite shape:

You think that you have never tried to do for yourself what Adam's hooked finger failed to do for you.

That is how, prudish, surprised, you put it, and your pulse is sudden and hot in your throat, followed by a gulp of acidic vomit, and the taste of soured milk. You cough, and your hands splay irregularly across the duvet, away from your body, and then back, held rigid, into the curve of your waist. But you know this, you think, and now it is different. You hold your mind firmly down; you keep it under control. This is how: you focus it back on the sea, watch as a single black-and-white wave jerks in towards an artificially-regular row of pebbles as though on war-time cine-film. It pulls out again, shivering at the edges, a mirage on hot tarmac but wet and real. More waves. The glory.

But then spreading like a slick of poisonous oil across the water, there is Adam's sharp breath, his bobbing eagerness, his voice ('did you come?') and the smell of burning pesto on the solid hob. You pull your breath in and you close off your mind. Again you feel sick. You tell yourself that you must not feel.

But then you know that that is not true. You are safe in the circle of your gentleman's love. You can relax just a little more. You can allow yourself the close-up which appears of Adam's bare crown, outlined irregularly by dark hair which has a chip-fat-greasy smell. You notice the shiny magazines on the floor. (Your stomach is tight at what you did not know.) You absorb through your pores the layer of human dust that has settled in the unventilated room. Then, tentative, gentle, you reach down your hand and begin through your rough pubic hair to massage at the loose section of skin that you feel there.

You are making an experiment and are not expecting much, so you are satisfied as you feel an increase in your body's heat and with that satisfaction you smile to yourself. You continue, concentrating hard, and slowly that concentration begins to draw down your pulse. You notice that your skin is becoming slippery, and that a smaller and smaller movement that you want to make is harder and harder to place exactly, but with each movement there is a reflex response to your hand which is becoming more immediate, closer, stronger. And so you are moving your hand more than you want and also breathing harder and your hips are hard-angled forward and their muscles pulled taut.

Cushioned on the gentleman's wine you are tipping towards being merely your body, but suddenly for a moment you are afraid that what you are doing is wrong and so you pull your hand back, slow your breathing and hear again the traffic outside the window and the drunken calls of men at closing-time, and then that worry too slips, skids away and in giving in to the temptation of holding yourself in that feeling, you have discovered the expedient of using your other fingers as well. You concentrate. You rub and you wiggle your fingers around. There is sweat too in the mess of your hair. Your breasts are suddenly tender to the touch of the sheets as though your skin is turned up high to feel them.

And what you feel is the start of a tremor which expands through your body out to your fingers but is tightening to a focus in a single knot of sense. Against your slippery fingers a muscular contraction like hard rings of rubbery squid and instinctively your knees come up and your torso curls forward to hold it. But then more than that a repositioning of your pulse into a hot, heavy beat that runs from a part of your body to which you have never even given a name up through your stomach and chest and down (as you stretch out to your full, taut length) into a tingle of released blood in your toes.

You lie there, surprised. Tears run backwards down your face and coldly into your ears, and your smile is the shape of the waves caressing the shore. (The glory.) Still lying, clothed, on your back, you bring your hand to your face. By the light of the streetlamps outside your open curtains you inspect your fingers' prune-shrivelled skin, smell their heavy sweat, taste their sharp, dry taste. And you think to yourself that you are a normal human being. That this is the high point of your life so far.

IX

You keep a little of that belief to yourself. But all the same you are eager to announce your love; and Sandy and Jenny want to hear. You sat together holding hands, you say, yeah, so romantic—looking at the sea. And then you went for dinner. That posh bistro on the waterfront, the one with the blue and white chairs. Mostly he talked. He walked you home, you tell them, and as you say that it feels right that he should have kissed you goodnight (Jenny would have been kissed goodnight), and so you tell them that as well. Your voice is warm with pleasure and anticipation.

But then all that day though you have promised that he will come he does not appear through the propped-open door. You hurry home to be there for him arriving and you watch TV and then, disappointed, you go to bed and you wake constantly through the night but still he is not there and nor does he come the next day, and you are surprised at his absence and you are in pain. Jenny tells you that you have to text him, says that otherwise you'll never know; and you will not admit that you don't have his number so you say instead that he does not reply.

'That's rubbish,' she says, 'pathetic,' and you defend him to her turned back, say he's busy, that he is a grown man with a full-time job after all. That actually he's not down here all of the time. That he works in Westminster, in London. Next to Big Ben. That he only comes for weekends. (And now it is already Monday. So that explains it, you say, and you allow yourself to feel relief though you know that it is no excuse.)

And with that reasoning Jenny is happier. She starts

again to ask you exactly what he said, she tots up what taking you for dinner must have cost. 'Not my type', she says, 'But if you fancy him...' and your smile is complicit because you have become adept at bringing yourself to a silent night-time climax (and so you know now every night that this passion is true).

And I agree with you. I agree that this is it. For what you have here is something we have not seen before. It is not only that you do not view this man with disgust (though both of us agree that is good). It is instead that you respect him; that he protects you; that (even at a distance) he gives you physical pleasures. So you need to have faith, that is all. It is, I note, only Tuesday, and Charles is an old-fashioned type. So do continue, my dear, to tell your tale.

You do.

The week passes. Then the weekend arrives and you turn down Baz's suggestion, by proxy, of a date. 'Thought you'd say no,' Jenny says, 'but I promised I'd ask. And it's not like you've got a date arranged.' You blush, and 'not yet' you say, but you are proud to say it for you know your gentleman can speak for himself. Then for all the hours that you are not in the café you stay at home despite the sun and you wait.

The following week your face is tired and pale. (The night-time shadows are stronger in your mind.) You get up each morning and you dress. You arrive at the café and Sandy greets you. With Jenny you go over again and again what you remember of what you said that night and what he might have thought you meant. You pretend again to text him, and then that you are surprised that you get no reply. And with every passing day that you lie to the two of them your tears are closer to the surface. You still make yourself come every night; but it is with increased sadness for still he is not there.

'So if he lives in London,' Jenny says on Thursday morning, 'what's he doing pulling down here?' And Sandy sees your mouth twist and 'hey, hon,' she says, 'you know she's only joking. I'm sure he's coming back.'

He brings himself down here, he told you, for quiet time on his own. You did not think to ask him why. When he was in front of you (wearing a proper ironed cotton shirt, suggesting what you order, pouring you wine) it did not matter that behind the glamour of his independent adult life the space was entirely blank. But now that space continues to grow and your face is tight and you do not smile.

Eventually Jenny loses her rag. 'Babe,' she says, 'he's a loser; you can't get hung up on him. Look,' she says, 'I'm off out tomorrow night. You should come. Baz is coming,' she says, and she winks and then she smiles. You say nothing. Then, 'whatever; if you want to go chasing a spineless weirdo...' and she turns away and you start to cry. And so in the end you agree to go. Just for a drink, she reassures you. Michelle will be there as well. No need for you to get off with him if that's not what you want. But, come on, let's have some fucking fun for a change.

X

On Friday night you leave work promptly and together, and with your wages in your pocket you hit the shops.

'Pretty rubbish,' Jenny says. 'All the same stuff. But we'll find something that'll make you look good.' You go as instructed into the changing room and she passes through dress after dress, then stands, hands on hips, biting her lip, assessing how you look. You do as you are told: you try more dresses, spin to show them off, show her the back view, spin again.

You buy the first thing that she declares will do ('You're amazing in that,' is what she says.) It is a dress. It is black and short and stretchy and you think it is a size too small. You also buy some black satin heels with a pink bow on the front. Then you go back to Jenny's to get ready.

The house is quiet and empty; her mum is out, 'Like normal. With Dominic. Her guy.' Upstairs Jenny's room is papered with flash photos taken in indistinguishable bars and with tear-outs of celebrities whose faces you can't place. The window looks out over a small, overgrown garden. The double bed is unmade, but the clothes on the floor are folded and not thrown. Jenny drops her shopping bags onto the bed. She crosses to the chest of drawers, sweeps the make-up pods off the top of the laptop and boots it up. She tunes automatically to the local radio: 'If you took a holiday…took some time to celebrate…'

'Right,' Jenny says and she rifles in the box under the bed and pulls out a bottle of supermarket vodka, takes a swallow and passes it to you. You do the same. And you try to relax and you smile.

'Just one day out of life…'

You take your new dress out of its bag and snap off the tag. You pull it on slowly, keeping on your tights. Then you slip your feet into the shoes, feel the heels tip forward your weight. You are shy that you're in her room, aware that getting dressed should be part of the fun, trying to spin it out.

'It could be, it could be so nice…'

You sit on the edge of the bed, drink some more vodka, admire and comment as Jenny tries on dresses and then a range of tops with a ragged-hemmed white denim mini. With each change, she looks into the floor-length mirror propped up by the door. You drink more vodka and you laugh at her pout. She turns and, 'Thank God,' she says, 'About time you smiled again.'

When she is dressed Jenny tops up her own make-up and then spends twice as long on yours. You watch her choose the colours for you, load the brush, tap off the excess powder. Then, 'close your eyes,' she says, and she sweeps her brushes across your eyelids and your cheeks. 'You've got great skin,' she says, 'Really consistent colour and no spots at all.' And you say 'Thanks.'

You reach the bar and the others are already there. You giggle as Baz asks if you want a drink and you too hug Michelle and exclaim at her clothes. 'Awesome,' you say, 'really cool,' and you laugh as she says 'and just look at you!' And Jenny is right; you have fun.

But your fate, I tell you, is a step ahead, because on Sunday morning as you are gossiping with Jenny behind the counter you look up and your gentleman is at the door. Abruptly you both are silent. But you notice as your body drops into tension and you are flooded with resentment and then you are depressed. He has walked over to you. He is embarrassed.

'Have you got a minute, Rachel?' he asks, and you mumble something and walk back across the room with him. (You see Jenny, recovered, making faces by the coffee machine, and Sandy holding back a laugh. You draw your focus back to your gentleman's face.) He has, he says, come down from London just to see you. 'Could we meet this afternoon?' he asks. (Ever the gentleman; of course he asks.) He has, he says, something that he thought he should say. Something that he has been turning over in his mind. A conversation, he says, that he'd rather have alone, just the two of you. Something he needs to clear up. You flush. And so does he. And he looks uncomfortable. You also are uncomfortable. You are due already to leave early today. You are going to the cinema with Baz. (Jenny has set you up with a proper date.) But you look at your gentleman and you see again the way his grey hair has been blown to one side by the wind, and you want to reach out and stroke it back into place. You cannot help your reaction, you say to yourself; he touches you physically as Baz does not. This, you say, is a sign of love. Serious, responsible, adult. A grand, a life-time, passion. He suggests that you meet at five on your bench outside. But you do not wish to be seen. You say, OK, but that you'll meet him down the prom. By the post-box, you suggest, and he assents. Then, 'I'd better get back to work,' you say. And he says, 'of course,' and he leaves.

You go through into the kitchen where Jenny is waiting. 'Told him to go away,' you say. 'No right to treat me that way.' And Jenny looks at you oddly and she is silent. Your heart races. You want to cry.

But you know, don't you, that you must hang onto what is right? That what you have been indulging yourself in with Baz is not something that is worth having? That the true treasure is in your love for this man whom you respect? You look up, and 'yes,' you say, 'of course.' And then your face is mischievous. 'That'll be Chaz,' you say, 'C-H-A-Z,' and, relieved, I look into your eyes and I smile.

XI

You leave work at four and Jan is in the hall when you get home. Her presence irritates you. You have time only to shower, do your hair and dress. You have taken to wearing lip gloss, the colour that Jenny smooths on repeatedly throughout the day. (You have not tried her heavy eyeliner; you shy away from its show of strength.)

'Good day?' Jan asks, and you force yourself to relax and you nod. 'Yes. Good'. You are still surprised and pleased at that response.

'Lucky you,' Jan says. 'God, you'd think from TV that a B&B's cash for no work. Like hell it is. I've not had a minute to myself, cleaning rooms, changing beds, on the computer dealing with the bookings. Bloody email.' The lines on her face form and reform like waves with every task she lists, as though the actions she lists live in the muscles under her skin.

You, less expressive, nod and then you frown in concentrated sympathy.

Jan is still spitting out words: 'A couple coming from Germany on Tuesday. Been on the phone three times today. "How far to the sea, please? " And what the temperature is like. Third time could I do packed lunches for them.' Then, 'Shit day,' she says. 'They happen. Glad yours was better.'

'Yeah. It was good', you say, and its goodness swells out from your heart and you feel your pulse beat in your fingertips. (This is the glory.)

'Oh, hang on a sec. Here,' Jan says, and she rifles through a pile of plastic-wrapped catalogues on the side by the grandfather clock and reaches out to hand you an envelope. 'This came this morning.'

'Oh,' you say. And with an immediate hot shot of confusion that derives from nothing conscious, 'OK.' Then, shaking your head, your stiff hand out, remembering yourself, 'thanks'.

You take it. (Nobody knows that you are here.) It is an A5 brown envelope, addressed in clean, straight, handwriting to Rachel Miller, 31 Seaview Court, Bournemouth. No postcode. (You do not recognise the writing. Somebody must know you are here.) You look down at it and your hands begin to shake. But then you look down at it more clearly and you realise, and rushing blood makes your cheeks mobile and your mouth expands into a smile. Of course, you think, you wouldn't recognise the writing. Almost nobody knows you are here. (He walked you to the very door.) You lift your face and smile your soft smile into Jan's eyes.

'Thanks very much,' you say to Jan, and leaving her disarmed in the hall you take the stairs and up into your room.

You close the door behind you and, like a film heroine, lean back against its gloss paint. It's funny, you think, but you wouldn't have guessed he'd write like that. You press your back against the wood and hug your elbows tight against your ribs. Firm, yes, but more stylish; slanting heavily, perhaps, and not these big round vowels. A hot thread runs down through your body and for an instant you close your eyes. Then you open them again, blink away the rainbows and with your right forefinger ease the envelope open and pull out the wedge of paper inside.

It is brown. It is another envelope. (Your brain gives an unexpected jolt.) You smooth your fingers across it, unfurling the battered corners. It, too, is addressed to you, to Rachel Miller, but at your flat back up North. And now there is a sharp pain across your temples and your head swings with faintness and you grip at the doorframe to hold your weight. You have turned it over, turned it away from your eyes, but still you feel sick and you see the shaking of a soaked umbrella and the Gollum face that turns up, grinning, to your own. You tear the flap open and drop the envelope, hard-crumpled, onto the floor.

The paper inside is pale blue. It is another envelope. It is dirtied and creased as though it has been passed from hand to hand, and it has been folded in half. You bend it back and open along the fold line. Your heart follows your brain and grows loud in confusion and your pulse radiates, fast and hot now, out to your hands—they are suddenly sensitive to the grain of the paper, to the ridges on the crease marks, to its cool feel against your skin. You look at the address and behind the paper you catch a tiny bird which flickers from its nest to the window and back. There are daisies on the windowsill, singsong dissonant through the long, long afternoon. A woman is screaming, is dragged along the corridor. The curtains are close around your bed.

You stop. And you force yourself to breathe. You look at your delicate hands holding the paper and look again at the address. This writing, you think, is different; it is more what you expect, a scrawl, slantwise, small-lettered across the envelope, with the postcode printed bold and clear. You tell your mind that you are confused. He did not, your brain consciously thinks, he did not know you then. But that thought brings with it no logical chain. The envelope gains weight in your shaking hands. Your growing response tells you that this is something to be afraid of, something you thought you had left behind. But still you feel the warm security of your gentleman's loving hand on your arm, and you remember your fingers rubbing, slippery, at that tiny knot of your kindling flesh. You jerk your fingers at the envelope, tear it open, tear out the paper inside.

It is a single, folded sheet.

'Dear Rachel', it says (and your heart bumps).

'Dear Rachel,

'I hope you are getting well again. I rang the hospital but they said that you'd gone and they'd forward the letter and I didn't have the address so I thought I'd try that. I hope it gets forwarded. I guess if you're reading it it has been. Just to say 'sorry' that I had to stop coming. It felt like I needed to give you space. I didn't want you to get the wrong idea if I kept on coming. I hope you didn't. It's just I thought that maybe you would. But Iris will have passed on my goodbye and best wishes, will have told you to text me when you were out. Just writing this as I'm surprised I haven't heard from you, but the hospital says you're not there anymore, so maybe you're too busy and everything's going well. I hope so. But just wanted to say so, and I haven't got your mobile or email so I've gone the old-fashioned route. You'll probably never get this. But even if you do I guess that's it. Give me a ring if you want – you've got my number; I just haven't got yours.

'Peter'

You swallow back the acid in your throat and read a second time. Lumpen, your brain gulps in the strings of poisonous words. Then it stops hard like wheels locked by sudden brakes. You lean on the door and your eyes take in the single sheet. It is nothing. Too flimsy to have survived its repeated transit, too short to have accrued the meaning you have given it. You stand there with it between your paper-skinned fingers. And all of a sudden you are life-endingly tired.

And your tale here has reached a full stop.

You are as though marble. I also stop. I stop, and I wait.

Then after a moment, listen, I tell you, you can call and call and people do not come. That is what the world is like. You call and he does not come. Just the same they do not come to me. That is how it is meant to be, what was intended from the beginning. He would leave you and say no goodbye, I tell you. I have not needed to force this: it is for you just as it was for me.

You are listening to me. You are silent. But then I can see you gather yourself. You breathe deeply once, in and out. And then here, now, with the energy you had at that moment you look up.

'You knew,' you say, and you are light-headed, near-faint with the pain of betrayal. 'You promised me,' you say, 'you swore.' Blood rushes to your face and your mouth twists and you bring up your hands and you cover your eyes.

And again we need to take a pause.

XII

We pause. For a while I mouth platitudes which you do not hear. Then we are both silent. You wrap your hands around your mug; your eyes are fixed on the sandy liquid it holds. I drink my tea; I read the magazines that are scattered around. The room around us fills and empties. Eventually you look up, and then you say, as though you need consciously to move every tiny contributory muscle in turn: 'Let...us...go...on.' And you know that with that you have given me something. I warm at the pleasure of your gift.

After a while you think you have recovered from your shock. You have crossed the room, placed Peter's note down on your bed and sat yourself down next to it. The paper slides into the dip you make in the mattress. You close your eyes. You are shaking gently. Your brain is lurching as though you are drunk. But you are holding on tight, forcing your thoughts down a logical track. Trying to think the logic through. How and why it has come. What it means to you now. (What he means; and you are faint, and then your body flushes in physical memory of a mindless cradled warmth. And you pull it back to the narrow salvation of logic.) How there is something that has changed.

But it is not that easy.

You are remembering your gentleman's hand on your arm, Baz's hands on your hips. And—with sudden fear that you cannot control your releasing mind—in a rush the drunken man who died in the road and Adam's pink face and the row of individual tears (you count them) along his jaw. You know you acted wrongly. (And your shoulders lock down and your calves are suddenly full of blood and your breath is shallow and tight.) You have done wrong. (And your heart contracts and you push down your rising fear with your logical, your brutal, mind.) You have done wrong. But you will not do it now. You will not (and you are stronger) do it to your gentleman. You will meet him today as you have planned. And you love him, and your stomach pulls in at the thought.

But though you try to tell yourself, firmly, that there is no reason why you should not go and in glory meet your gentleman now, what you tell yourself now has no meaning. Logic does not work. Words which you normally would pick straight up are suddenly harder to find. (The glory is a shape of breath and no word.) Your interior sentences begin to pause, to cast around, to end in a way which was not how they were when they began. I need to go because, you say, and you pause, and you do not know what because is, and so you guess that it is love that drives you, or tiredness, or the need to see a friend, and all the time you know that there is no because, that you are swimming in something blank.

I want to see, you say—then pause—I want to go, I want to be. And as you hesitate the taint deepens. Words begin to elide. You start to say 'you', but it is now 'your'. 'Shoe' becomes 'snow' and 'the sky' is now 'the starlings'. After a while you believe you are falling into another world. Snow is as good as shoe for neither (from neither) is what you mean (or need). The connections your mind formed when you were a child are being loosened not just against your will but without its awareness at all. Something is impelling you to pick up your bag which is now a pad, or it is 'not a pad', which, if you allow for that swerve in the road (or rood), makes more of the old world type of sense. It is not that your mind is more colourful (or comfortable) or artistic (or artisan); it is that every start of a sentence is diffusing its energy where once it was arrow-straight, and the being that is yourself in the back of your head is left standing with the verb in its hand looking at a multifarious multitude of words as likely as each other to be the one that comes next, all equally true or not to what you have forgotten that you meant to say.

You begin to succumb to the magic, watching like a sick child with a kaleidoscope, twirling a changing view of the world where all results are equally good, equally solid, equally beautiful, equally true. But behind the flood of words you find a rising distress that who you are is floating away. And then that something which is human meaning common to Jenny, Sandy, Baz, your gentleman, something which has been moored in your mind since you learned to speak as a child is suddenly un-tethered and is nodding on the sea, bobbing on the sun, batting on the breeze, bowling through the back-streets. That the land has disappeared and you are alone in this place or face or gaze where words are bit or not what they were and meaning too is slipping away.

You are by necessity there alone.

You turn to the wall and you lie your body down. Something inside you is exercising a pull inwards, a focussing of the sensation that was in the outside of your face into your throat and down into the depths of your chest. With it your thoughts begin to fade; they follow your muscles and skin into collapsed formlessness. A fog steals up from the top of your spine, splits in two at the back of your neck, and its soft-edged pincers curve symmetrical round the top of each ear until they meet in your forehead and drift down your face like rain streaked down a window pane. You can sink into the wordlessness of where you are. It is greyish white, and inside its embrace you fall away.

You lie there.

You know enough to know to keep yourself in this soft fog. (It offers the best chance that you will survive.)

You hear the echo of a tolling bell.

There are voices outside the window. They are labelling drought-shrivelled flowers.

They are by your side, are opening your elbow for the needle, are gripping tight at your arm.

You move your distant hand and the grip fades. You feel your brain stutter; you move your hand again. Your fingernails catch on roughness. The pads of each finger awaken the counterpane. Your concentration sharpens and beyond the roughness a tessellation of hexagonal colours gathers strength. That tessellation goes with the grandfather clock in the hall below your room. Your mind latches onto its rhythm, hears it three, four, five times. Deep inside you something flickers and you know this should have meaning but then as you open your mind to hear it a streak of panic rises through your spine and you push your reaction down and away and you press your mind also down, back into the fog.

But then the flicker is more insistent. You are more sure that the chiming clock has a meaning to you even though now it is silent and nothing has changed. And then with sudden energy you remember that you will see your gentleman today, and then that you are late. And without a thought for your hair, with no smooth slick of pink lip-gloss, you are out of your room, down the stairs, out through the front door, running down the street towards the front.

Late afternoon is primetime in town and you are overwhelmed by faces and faces and backs of heads all meandering along on holiday time. They are pink with the sun, shiny, creased with sweat runnels and spotted with chocolate ice-cream. Their hair is wet from the sea, is pulled tightly into dripping ponytails and tufted by the wind, is 'done' but becoming disarrayed. Like animals being gently herded they slow to graze at the stalls or on views of the sea, then ease themselves forwards again, reshaping the wandering crowd. It is busy and they are packed tight together as, shoulder-first, you bump and bump against them. Panic is rising again in your mind, and with it a horror that you will be paid back for what you have done, that you do not deserve what you have, that what you have will be taken from you.

You come up against a large, mousy woman in a sweat-stained pink shirt and khaki shorts who is searching through the spinning postcard stands whilst behind her her impatient husband rocks back and forward on the edge of the pavement. You shudder with adrenalin. Your mind bites itself down. You push on forwards.

In the road the cars are bumper to bumper as the tourists leave at the end of the day. Tired, impatient, their drivers ease themselves with every movement as far as they can go, and so though this pavement is full you cannot get between them and over to the other side, and that side is full too and you are hobbling with one foot on the pavement and the other in the rubbish in the gutter. Then suddenly you are face-to-face with a family and they cannot step back onto the pavement out of your way and nor can you and anyway they are reddened by the sun and in no hurry. The children are eating ice creams, looking down, licking the drips carefully off their fingers, and their

hair is tousled and 'please' you say, 'please', and the mother
looks surprised at the tears in your eyes, and, apologetic,
slow, she hustles them to one side. You are so close to the
hot cars that you brush them as you pass but then there is
a space and you are through it and you burst out at the far
side of the crowd and only the sea is in front of you.

You stop and you pant and, unseeing, you switch your
head from side to side. There are people, too many people;
and he,—you force your eyes into focus—he is not here.
And for a moment panic tears at your throat, but then, 'the
post box' you remember and dodging, running, searching
for the familiar profile you trip and stumble along the busy
prom. You get there. You stop and you heave in breath. You
are wild. You are swallowing back tears. It is half-past five
and he is not (he is not) here.

Your heart thumps with fear, with guilt, and your vision
swims and then—ah, as your thought drops into place—
you feel the remnants of glory, and you know that he has
gone to the café to find you. Your brain lights up again and
again you have a direction which propels you through the
crowds.

You are breathless as you arrive and swing the door
sharply open. Eyes alight with hope you look around the
customers, waiting to see his thick grey hair, the brown of
his coat. Then you pause and look again, more slowly. And
then, heavy-headed, you switch your gaze to behind the
counter where Sandy is standing, looking surprised.

'You OK?' she asks. 'Wasn't expecting to see you back
again today. Thought you were out with Baz; but clearly
not.'

'What,' you say, confused, 'what.' (You are still
absorbing that he is not here.)

'I thought this would have to wait till tomorrow,' she

says, and with a complicit smile that remembers the buoyed excitement of your declared love she brings her hand out from behind her back and flourishes an envelope towards you.

'Not from Baz,' she says and hands it over.

Your heart leaps. You jerk your fingers at the envelope, tear it open, tear out the paper inside.

It is a single, folded sheet. 'Dear Rachel', it says,

'Dear Rachel,

'Sorry for the scribble and that I missed you today. Don't know whether you were around and we just couldn't spot each other or whether you couldn't make it. Either way maybe for the best.

Actually I'm not going to be here again; I've had the time I needed on my own. On that note, I wanted too to thank you. My wife and I since our daughter died, we've needed time apart. I told you how alike you are to my— to our—poor dead daughter. That you reminded me so touchingly of her from the first time that I saw you by the pier. It has given me new strength to spend time with you. I hope that you have enjoyed our conversations too. I am sorry they must come to an end. I think it's best if we don't stay in touch. I hope that everything will be OK for you.

'Sorry again I couldn't hang around today. But probably as I said for the best.

'Charles'

'Bad news?' asks Sandy, and, separate, withdrawn, you automatically shake your head. You feel sick. 'Sure you're OK, honey?' she says. 'You do look awfully pale. Can I make you a cup of sweet tea?'

'No, I'm fine,' you say, moving towards the door. 'Got to meet someone.'

She is still looking after you, telling you to take care as

you get outside and disappear into the crowd.

But the energy that propelled you out of the café takes you only the first ten steps and then you stop. You are confused, exhausted; nothing now tells you where you should go. You are afraid that Sandy will come out and find you, and that helps you get round the corner. But that is all, and so you find you are moving directionless and at the speed of the meandering holidaymakers. You do not see them. You have become aware of a boulder in your mind. It has dimensions and weight though your mind does not. It is crushing all of your ability to think.

You drift through the crowd. You look alternately left at the sea and right towards the town.

Gradually you become aware of a single thought solidifying in your mind: you know you must find him and that you must—you must—explain.

XIII

You return to Jan's house and slide unnoticed through the hall, up the stairs and back into your room. You take out your suitcases. Into the small one you place a change of clothes, your scarf (he said you were beautiful!), your toothbrush, your hairbrush and a deodorant. Then you fold everything else you own into the larger one, zip the lid and place its bulging bulk tidily at the end of your bed.

With precision (your brain is surprisingly clear) you write a note that thanks Jan for her hospitality and explains you need to leave unexpectedly. You fold up in it the rent you owe her and place it on the case. Then, exhausted, you lie down.

You cannot rest.

Your brain is spinning at double or at triple speed in a tight molecular ball just next to your head. This acceleration of your brain towards a seething black hole is something which is new; in it the thoughts are moving faster than you can catch hold of them to focus, to change, or even to know their direction, until they have become a blur of somebody else's meaning and that is unbearable and needs to be dulled. And so you force your concentration away from the blur: but then you picture all the people the promenade holds and yet among all the faces he, he is not there, and so you close your eyes tight and you begin to shudder from the stomach out, rolling shudders like childbirth pains, and you are crying and hot and you grip your knees so tight you bruise yourself and that pulls you back to tonight and this room, but that acknowledgement only takes you to a place from which your momentum leaves you further to fall. Your head fills with the need to cause yourself pain so that at least you feel, and you beat at your arms and your chest and your head, then you are past that and all you can do is give in, see the red behind your eyelids, dissolve your brain in the image of your body streaming with blood.

(Your eyes are closed, your brain detached from your body. You are distant from the stimulus of your bedroom's world.)

The hours pass. Perhaps you sleep. Then once again your eyes are open.

The window is paler against the wall.

You lie and try to let your mind absorb the day. You try to let your shoulders relax. You try to feel the night retreat. You feel better, you tell yourself, because it is morning and therefore your mind is clear. And so silently, silently you get up from your bed, pick up the small suitcase, and leave the house.

Before it is even fully light you are on the London train.

XIV

You are confined in safety there, so I will leave you for a moment. That may seem cruel; it is not. To understand what happens to both of us next you need to know me better, to know what has happened since you left me in the hospital on that autumn day. What has happened and why.

My first discharge I have already described (I thought then that it would be the only one). Back to the house I loved, though to find his family and his silence. The dress, perfumes, unconsciousness, blood. The shame then of being back on that ward. Perhaps you can imagine. Despite the drugs, nurses on shifts full-time by my bed. A bulbous one during the day. Black moles on her face. Heavy. Flung her weight over me as I woke, flailing, from what they had given me. Pinned me down as I fought for breath and for space, hit the panic button by my bed and they all came in and I fought them and they smothered me and again with that needle they forced me back into the shadow lands. Again. Again. Until I had no more strength and I could fight no more—and then when I woke, a different one by my bed. Reading aloud the horoscopes. You will meet someone who will end up meaning more to you than you can imagine now. Between star-signs I was unconscious. Or I felt unconscious though I was awake and I could see. The world was a hand's breath too far away for me to reach it, for me to live in it as I knew the rules decreed. I tried, I promise you, to keep my standards up, but even then something was slipping away. I was dirty as you were. I too had clotted hair. I still wore that dress (they had brought me nothing else) but it was creased, blood-spotted, smelt of hospital roast dinner, of sweat, of spilt tea. Locked up there, isolated, held imprisoned, I struggled to hold myself appositely for Lady Buchanan. But I had nothing to put in her place. So it made sense when the doctor came to me with a nurse behind him like the Grim Reaper with a syringe and not a scythe in his hand. David, they told me, was filing for divorce, and the two of them and the one who was already there by my bed, they watched how I reacted, and I looked through them and, glassy-eyed, smiled at your Van Gogh beyond. 'Oh,' I said, as though he had deserted me already. 'Oh,' I said, and I did not cry.

It was because of the impending divorce, you see, that when I was discharged again home was now the London flat. What was to have been the Buchanan London flat, I should say, for none of us had ever lived there before. When I left the hospital that is where the pre-paid taxi went. I arrived and it was cold and it was empty except for furniture battered by the tenants who had left the previous week. There were fat brown legal envelopes blocking the door. I stacked them unopened on the work surface, out of the way. They had told me, you see, that I had to try. They had assisted me in setting my goals. Nothing too ambitious, they warned, and plenty of time to rest. So my aim, my raison d'être, for the foreseeable future was to attain a safe routine: up in the morning and a shower and dress (I had learned again to do that in the hospital before I left). I had coffee at the chain round the corner, lunch with the paper in another coffee shop and went window-shopping in the afternoon. Then I cooked a proper dinner (nutrition, they said, is key), washed up and sat in front of the TV until it was time for my pills and for bed.

That was all clear enough. And initially it seemed to work. I did as I had planned. I opened the boxes of my clothes that had arrived. I had my hair done. I carried myself well in the street (I checked in shop windows as I walked.) And as planned at first the people stayed away. But there was a flaw in the routine that we had not foreseen. For though I rang the changes as often as I could, the coffee shop staff came to recognise me, knew what I would order, wanted to say hello. So though, as agreed, I did not call, they increasingly came to encroach on my world. And then I saw that they were not the only ones. Sturdy policemen were on the pavement outside my front door; and men in suits telling people what to do. At lunchtime and in the evening the streets were crowded beyond bearing, and at night they came with relentless persistence. At first I kept safe just with a chair back against the front door as I slept. But as the days passed and they grew angry they became more insistent, and it took more of my time and I needed to cover the windows as well as the door. But it was all OK; this was all that was wrong. And I did not call. And the sofa against the front door was enough to hold them back, then with the dining table against the big drawing-room window with the chairs on top I would hear the clatter as they broke in, and the armchair against the other window. In the bedroom I pushed the bed under the window-sill and if I lay on it and stayed awake I was safe from that direction too.

Every day as the light grew in the grey sky I sat up from sleeplessness and shifted the furniture into place. I did it in case daylight guests came (in case when I called for them they came—for now I admit I had begun again to call), and then no-one came and at night I shifted it back so all apertures were safe. But even with every entrance blocked against them their voices filled the air. Hold her back, they said. And, it must be someone's fault. And what the fuck have you done. You're ill, they said. How could you be so stupid. Let us look after you. You stupid, self-centred bitch. Hold her down; pass that needle. They've gone, they've gone. They will not come. (They will not, I whispered, come again.)

I turned up the radio as high as it would go, sat beside it keeping it going through all the dark hours. I learned the local advertisements by heart, repeated them to myself as I went back and forth checking the windows until the light came again, but the voices came and they came until the rattling and knocking at the door turned into a bang and someone swearing behind the sofa. Then there was nothing I could do and they held me down and though, unladylike, I screamed and I fought I felt them pull up my skirt and stick the needle in and then still they held me down and then again there was nothing except the hospital, and when I came out again not even the flat keys were there.

And so, my dear, I understand. For I also, I am destitute, and I also am alone.

But (you say it, you are right) I do go on. And it is your story that we are telling here. So, let us continue.

LONDON

I

You are on the train to London. You have rid yourself of your night terrors and now your mind feels light, as though at any minute it might blow away. Yet you are strong. You remember that you have a purpose. (Remember that you must find him.) You remember also that you have felt like this before, but that you have been able to help yourself. You remember that what you need is continued concentration on something unquestionably real. You place both hands palm down on your knees and press down, as hard as you can.

It works. What appears in your head is a sensible, adult reaction to the situation. What you see is Sandy and Jenny. Sandy will have been called by Jan, you think. And there will be a sense of surprise, of shock that you are not there. Sandy will be angry. I knew, she'll say, there was something wrong. But to walk off just like that—and you see her anger mix with concern and be overwhelmed by the practicality of what the fuck we do now. And Jenny will look worried and she'll say that she liked you, and that she thought you and Baz had a chance. In the distant reaches of your mind they flounder under emotion which once again you can only see from the outside. Which now means nothing to you.

And you are filled with guilt that all along as you bantered, as you danced, as you flirted with Baz; as you listened to Jenny prattle and warmed at Sandy's care; that all along you were a fraud. That you never told them the truth of who you were, and why you had come, and that it was inevitable you would leave because all along you were someone else.

What you know is that you can never go back.

You shudder at that thought. But you cannot allow it to take hold. So with your right hand you take a pinch of skin on the back of your left; you dig your nails in; you breathe. You become a mere observer of your realisation that you always knew your seaside life was a fantasy, that candyfloss and waves were not enough. And you see outside the window that this is the sort of day when the sun shines out of the mist like a colourless moon.

You see that, and you close your eyes. And behind your eyelids and beyond the pain in your hand the fire and the heat are gone and there are only blank thoughts marching through your head like strings of cut-out paper men. (They will be your salvation.) You release the pinch of skin on your hand, and focus on the men (away from the waterfront; away from the sky). You are intrigued by their precision and by their nothingness. They are hard-edged figures, identical, opaque and entirely blank. But then, as you watch, the fibres of their paper connections come apart, and they grow faces and they begin to walk in opposite directions and in different ways. Some hurry, arms wrapped tight around themselves, urgent and directed. Some are waiting, paused, in the middle of the space. One is kicking at a white leather-clad ball. They form and re-form into variously-shaped crowds of thousands on a busy shopping street. You watch the patterns develop as though through a kaleidoscope. But then smoothly, gently, with no hint of change, washing through them all like the close-ranked, multi-piercing, deadly hail of a line of medieval archers are knives coming down in their hundreds out of the sky. They are flick knives, the length of a hand, bent at the handle but travelling straight, with a purpose, as though thrown hard by everyone in your sight though no-one is pulling out the blades, opening them, swinging them out and letting go. And they are real. They are lodging deep in the fat and muscle of the no longer-paper people, creating steel angles against the human bodies' curves. These people are pierced from all directions though they do not bleed. Yet still they are merely wandering and still at the varied speeds at which they moved when you first saw them. There is no reaction. Nothing has changed.

One of the forms is coming directly towards you. His eyes are ringed with black eyeliner and inside that burnt-out hole they are pale and blank. He has a blade woven through his face, going in through his right cheek and out through his pink-glossed lip. There is no blood, no evident pain, just a grey face with smudged eyes and a more grey blade. He is walking closer to you out of the mist, and closer, the sun pale over his shoulder. You are directly on his path and the space in the scene which is you is only a space and cannot move away. As he reaches you—at the point at which he and his knife must overwhelm you with meaningless existence, must simply become your body—you realise in a moment what it is that you know: the world is a place where mere cruelty is the baseline of existence; that that is the way it has been and the way it should be, and these people are all right, that there is no reason to care, no reason to react. And the thought grows into a halo of light, acquires meaning as though it is solid and you can touch it.

And so you open your eyes. You have come out of the mist and you can see the view around you. You see the swelling of the South Downs out of the fields, but cloud is drifting on their slopes and so you are as though holding a lantern in the middle of the mist and what you see is a dreamscape, bleached out.

You look again, range your gaze around you from side to side. And there, in the opposite seat, is a man sitting silently, pierced with tens of knives. He is smiling beatifically at the view outside which is passing, untouchable, behind glass at one hundred miles per hour.

For the first time now you are afraid. Holding yourself tight you press your back harder into the seat. The passengers around you are all too close, as though each is in an invisible viscous bubble and those bubbles jostle and bounce against each other, rebalance their weights and move on, but you have no bubble and so you are bare and defenceless against their movement. You are afraid of their proximity, a beaten child cringing into the corner of the room, putting sheer distance from the door, drawing tightly away from its captor though that captor is nowhere around. But then you arrive at a solution. You do not feel your face retreating into white, but you recognise where your mind is going and you do not stop it. It is focusing deep inside onto a single point, deliberately relaxing the outer muscles to free your blood for that internal pull. You are drawing the blood in from your limbs, forcing it into a single channel which points forwards with no flexibility, and with no window out onto the world. As you move towards it your breathing slows, becomes more shallow. Moving to where you are going there is little need for oxygen; your direction is nothingness. Your limbs start to lose sensation; unmoving they lose the sense of location, or proximity, or space. You are slipping into a void in which there is no space. Though you have to concentrate to start with to get there you know that there will come a point where all of that concentration is the last thing left in your mind and then it too will drop away and leave you suspended. You will continue to patrol the borders, continue to pull blood away from limbs that want to feel, extremities that are touched and want automatically to react, but with enough concentration you know you will be held and your being will swell into whiteness, and then you will be home.

That is where you now go. You close your eyes against the bubbles and the knives and the night and the colourless sun, and you pull back into the whiteness you still know how to access and which you deeply trust.

But you are not to be allowed to go there. You are perplexed. You have begun your preparations, but whenever you reach for the final switch on your patrolling mind you begin again to feel. The train is jerking into and out of a station. There is an announcement about sandwiches and then about arrival times. The man next to you is listening to headphones which emit a distinctive beat which you cannot relinquish. Someone is eating salt and vinegar crisps. You stay still, eyes closed, and you shrink from your reality, but all the same you are retained in the world; this is where you now have to be.

You are surprised. You are afraid.

You stay there.

Eventually the guard announces you are approaching the final station and you force yourself to open your eyes. It takes effort, a conscious focus on holding your eyelids off their natural closed curve. And at first there is no reward. What you see is stained concrete blocks with burnt out windows leering over the dirty rails. You blink at them, blink, blink. Their desolation reaches into you with the beginning of claws; it takes all of your effort to look away. First, to the buildings next to them, smart apartment blocks with balconies glassed in against the noise of the trains. Then to blank offices, a glimpse of the river, more apartments, the river again.

Another train eases past, blocking your view. It is faster than you, and then slower, and then faster again and inside it the same blank faces pass you back and forth like a J-cloth polishing hard at stainless steel. You feel dizzy. You swallow. You turn and look individually at the closer faces of your own carriage preparing themselves for arrival and beyond them and out of the far window. You understand that you are still moving forwards. You shake the sickness out of your head. Then on your side you move ahead again of the stream of red carriages.

Now landmarks are swinging into view against the still-early morning mist. Your attention is snatched and held by the massive Wonderland-wheel of the London Eye and by the Lego-blocked buildings at its foot. Then the warm, ornate towers of Parliament are there and you breathe deeply at their familiarity. They disappear and then are briefly there again. Your brain struggles to place them geographically on the same plane as the wheel, the flat water and the Lego. But you lock onto their direction in your mind, and knowing they are there tells you where you need to go. You relax a little. You allow yourself to breathe. Above you, half-seen, a flag flutters on the top of the Shell building.

II

The train stops, the doors open, and in that instant everyone around you reveals a strong purpose. Men and women alike march away down the platform, varying in their speeds as high heels click and wobble, trainers are held back on awkward chopstick legs by skirts tight round the knees, legs padded and trousered stride out with briefcases bumping against them. For convenience you leave your suitcase on the train, and join them. Individually people rush to overtake, their laptop cases swinging wide with momentum; or they hold back, fiddling with straps on their bags, heads down, but feet still shuffling forward. Collectively the competent crowd reshapes itself en masse around expected obstacles—a mini rubbish lorry, locked skips, benches at knee-height and then a tall vending-machine. Then it splits apart. Mostly it funnels down the steps into the Tube. But holding still in your mind your image of the ornamented Parliament, you instead follow the other part through the barriers, through the slippery concourse and out of the station.

Now with more space the stream of people spreads further. You stay with the largest group. Dammed then released by the traffic lights, it surges across the road at the bottom of the station entrance, passes under the railway arches and climbs the steps behind the building labelled in clear blue letters 'Royal Festival Hall'.

(The people and the buildings tell you you are reaching towards the centre of the world. That this is the route on which you will find your gentleman. That this is London and that the answer must be here.)

You pass a bust of Nelson Mandela, pass cafés filled with fast-talking breakfasters. And then you see the river in front of you and you take a deep breath. You begin to dawdle against the speed of the suit-clad men and women. You are drawn towards the water. Absenting yourself for a moment from the flow of life, you stand by the railings, lean against them, watch the high river moving steadfastly past. Its matte surface is grey like ruffled concrete.

You ignore the crowd climbing up again above you to the bridge and then trotting away towards the arched hall of Charing Cross, towards Trafalgar Square, towards Covent Garden and the West End, towards Haymarket, Regent Street, the Strand, Whitehall and the Mall.

Instead, remembering his voice, remembering his description of his view of Big Ben, you focus your eyes on the Houses of Parliament ahead, and you walk slowly left along the riverbank.

With every step you take something is locking down inside you. You are becoming rigid with preparation. But then there are flashes of emotion that impale your mind: 'I wanted to thank you,' a voice says inside you, and 'it has given me new strength to spend time with you,' and 'I hope that you have enjoyed our conversations too,' and you smile across the whole of your face. But then 'my wife...my poor dead daughter...must come to an end' and your face is immobile and your confused limbs creak as you walk.

You move on. You move forward.

III

A woman is sitting begging at the south end of Westminster Bridge where the steps up from the Embankment reach the higher level of the road. Her head is at knee-height to the rush hour army. Like an unwatched child deep in concentrated make-believe she has folded in her thin limbs and her head is bent over. She sifts dark coins from her hands to her spread purple shawl. And again. And again. She listens hard for their click and tinkle above the rhythm of hundreds of smart footsteps. She is oblivious to where the footsteps are going and to why it matters to them to go there so firmly. She does not look up. And the commuters in turn do not see her. They do not need to: each set of feet merely follows the one in front so the whole mass together moving feet behind feet like a swaying Chinese dragon absorbs the bulge of her presence on the bridge and then, relaxed, fans out again beyond her.

You are still a part of that crowd as it marches up the steps. But now that it has been funnelled off the wide Embankment and onto the pavement your hesitation marks you as out of place. You feel hustled, then confused, then hunted. You notice your pulse is radiating irregularly from your chest. You are jostled as a man overtakes, and then the woman behind him. Your eyes are focused tight on the narrow strip of pavement you need to see in order not to fall. Everything else is formless around you; you are ignoring the formlessness. You, too, pass the destitute woman without seeing her.

You walk on. You arrive at the middle of the bridge—you check back to confirm it is the deepest middle— you stop. You are looking down. The water is still grey. Heavy ripples pushed out by the bridge supports mark slants firm as girders across its surface. The whole is vast and it is solid. It reaches into your gut. It does what you need: as you stare into it everything around you becomes flimsy, transient, unreal. (Commuters begin to glance at you as they pass.) Your hearing fades into white noise, and your peripheral vision into mere colours. That is what you want. And so you continue to lean on the balustrade, and you continue to look down. The water is as dark and all-absorbing as you have needed. Unlike the sunlit sea it carries no hope, spawns no life. It is matched exactly to what you now are. And so you allow yourself to be dizzy against its movement, allow yourself to rock forwards from your heels.

But though you rock forward and let your hands take your weight on the balustrade you are not fully seduced by this moment; for despite your absorption in the formlessness, the transience, the inhuman movement, despite your attempted loss of yourself, there is still something active in your brain. You pause. You listen to it. And you remember: you have a purpose here in this city, and it is not yet fulfilled. You feel again in your body the decision you made in the Bournemouth crowd. You know that it was right (that you must). It leaves you no choice. And so, though with effort, you lift your view from deep in the river to its surface, and then from that surface to the buildings which crust the banks. You breathe deeply, once, in and out. Then you turn back to the flowing crowd. Nothing has changed.

(Your breath comes more easily at that no change.)

The mass of people continues to pass, the system continues to function. You do your duty and look for his features in every face. Your eyes twitch across the range of your vision as you check that he, that he, that he, is not the one you're waiting for. You begin to relax at your lack of success, concentrating less on each face in turn. But then that face (you check again), that face is him: only paces away he has appeared. And your stiff mouth cries out, 'Charles!' and he looks sideways out of the locked down vision of the crowd and he sees you and he stumbles and his unique face is bloodless with shock and fear.

You do not notice. You are stunned; you had not expected him to come. You are here, and you are fulfilling your duty to a force you don't understand, but nonetheless his arrival is a reality which you cannot absorb. You turn your head faster from side to side, scanning the thousands of people in your sight, wondering how he and you can have been pulled together here when on the Bournemouth waterfront you were so far away. How it was that your body knew where to be. How your mouth which could not speak could call his name. But then you focus your eyes onto his face. He is talking; you can see his lips move.

'My daughter,' he is saying, 'so much like you. But then she died. A car crash. Two months ago. I thought I'd made myself clear; didn't want you to misunderstand. I needed time on my own to think. Though I enjoyed our conversations. But I didn't mean—I mean, I wasn't thinking of you that way. You didn't think that, did you? My wife, I couldn't talk about it with my wife. It pushed us apart.'

He is explaining something, you think to yourself, and it means something to him and you do not know why, because he is here, in the flesh, and so there is nothing he needs to say.

'She had hair just like yours,' he is saying, 'And your smile. And she so loved the sea when she was small.' And

225

though he tries to smile it does not reach his eyes.

But it does not matter because with his arrival you are merely curious. As you stand and he talks and you do not hear, your curiosity is blossoming into a conclusion. He is not dapper, you say to yourself, and you are proud of what you feel and see. Instead he is afraid. Your beloved gentleman,—you peer closely at him, and you see wind-blown grey hair, and emerging liver spots, and a dirty mark on his mackintosh arm—your gentleman is a coward; he cannot not make you whole.

(You are light-headed. You grip the balustrade behind you. Your eyelids come down to form their lock-tight seal. You sway.)

He is still talking. 'But can I do anything for you?' he is saying, 'What can I do?'

You are surprised. You open your eyes. You shake your head. 'There is nothing you can do,' you say, with deliberate clarity. 'I do not love you. I do not need anything from you.' And you remember a woman with a pearl ring for sorrow and remember that she made you tea and handed you tissues and that she sat with you and heard you talk and wrote your story down.

You watch his face pull down against the relief threatening to rise in his eyes. 'If you're sure,' he says, and he looks at his watch. (He does not read the time.) 'Look,' he says, 'any time you need help—' and he pulls out his wallet, takes a sharp-edged business card from it and, 'all my details,' he says, and you still do not understand but nod all the same, and say 'thanks'.

Then he turns, takes a step away and is instantly absorbed back into the commuting crowd in which he belongs. You do not bother focussing your eyes to watch him disappear.

But though the concept of him staying was meaningless, with his departure everything has changed. You are no longer waiting for something to happen; not even a part of you is waiting, expecting, hoping. Instead you exist only in this present: standing on the bridge, holding onto the balustrade, looking down into the water. Now your concentration is absolute and there can only be one conclusion and so you take your time and relax into the flow. The water continues to move by below you and you are transfixed as though you are a child playing pooh sticks on a humped sandstone bridge over a splashing village stream. The commuters behind your back disappear. You do not move your head from side to side, do not inspect the slim, rubbished beaches that the tide has revealed, do not watch the boats as they ride the slopping waves. Instead you stand there and settle into what is meant to be, and you see the grey water, and your hands scrape on the rough stone, and you feel as though something is growing inside you, as though there is a pressure that increasingly you cannot keep down, as though who you are is no-one anymore and something is going to burst inside you and then you will be nothing and you do not need to care. There is no will inside you anymore to fight against the bursting, and so it swells to take up the whole of your stomach, and your lower back and your chest. And then with sudden terror you try to hold it down, try to lock your throat against its roaring rise, bend your body over and splay your hands.

In the moment that you pause, looking down, the vision of a summer afternoon river cruise passes under the bridge. The deck is packed tight with tourists in shorts and sweatshirts, heavy cameras cutting into their fleshy shoulders. At the prow is a Japanese woman in a plastic poncho, consulting the guidebook in her hand. There are jostling teenagers in sparkle-encrusted jeans with home-dyed hair, elderly couples hunched against the wind, and two shivering women trying to look relaxed in flippy summer dresses and pale sling-back kitten heels which catch in the decking. One of them is wearing my ring. Universally the adults are following the pseudo-cockney commentary from the stern, looking as instructed at the Houses of Parliament, identifying the terrace of the Upper House where the perfect afternoon tea is underway beneath open-sided marquees (envying the patrician clink of champagne flutes and the fleeting air-kisses). Behind them, on the left side of the cruiser, there are two children standing on the seats looking at the other boats, looking down for fish in the water, pointing out shadows and ripples to each other.

And you know that what you are seeing is in another time and another world. Because now you are here and it is morning not afternoon and you are locked into the rippling frame that is all of your vision. It is the end; all feeling of the world is gone; you are drunk on the flow of the water. (There is a splash, and then another splash and the boys who were scuffling on the cruiser have disappeared, and the woman with the pearl ring was not watching them, and did not see them go.) And in your drunkenness you are spiralling in and down to the eye which is 'I' which is the self you have kept hidden, protected, the grain at the centre of who you are kept apart for all those years. And at that purity in the eye is the view of a child who saw something that she could not bear. And for the split of a second she is there and bathed in light, and then you swing with vertigo and the sky tips up and the buildings follow its pull. Your vision is crowding into your head in jostling coloured blocks that are fighting with the night for space and in your ears a sound is ringing, ringing. You close your eyes and behind your eyelids is hiding the orange of the exploding urban sky.

Below on the cruiser the world is turning upside down. Hold her, hold her, they shouted, and it was me in my flippy dress that they held onto, and 'quick' they shouted and the world exploded around me in crowds and sirens and horns. The policemen asked how old were they and I didn't know. He asked for my husband, for his name and a number to contact him. I didn't know. And then some woman in the background began to scream: 'I don't know, I don't know, I don't know!' she cried and I shook at the sound and held my arms out to her and she screamed and they held me back and I called and called to my darling boys and still there was no reply.

You lean forwards and your fingernails scratch at the rough stone and despite everything pain rises inside you out of your hands and behind the sound of the people you hear the wash of the river against the bridge supports and the wing-beats of the wheeling gulls below. And then for a moment your brain relaxes a fraction and another sound moves in from behind your ear. And 'I beg you darling' says the sound.

I beg you, it says. Listen. Listen to me. And you hear it and then you lurch away and the world tips again on its hinge and your bleeding fingers press down harder and your calf muscles tense so you are ready to fall. But then the voice is there again; it is speaking out of the gripping pain in your arm. 'It will be OK,' it says, and you are rigid against it. And then you hear it begin to sob. 'O God,' it cries out, 'O God, I can't help. I'm calling, calling and you won't reply.'

But then something becomes detached in the narrative

which has taken over your head, and you look down and you open your eyes. The pain is coming from the hand on your arm; a hand with thin fingers, dirty fingernails and a large pearl ring. Your stomach distends with the shape of a memory and as the pain says 'darling, darling, come to me' you close your eyes again and swallow hard against the beat of your heart which is becoming all that you are.

Because behind your eyelids your soul is swirling in a shattered wave of darkness and life. You writhe at its centre. You know that you are lost. You abandon life. But with your heart-beat it is as though your self is insisting on reasserting itself. And then as your mind threatens disintegration into molecular darkness instead a brass-edged porthole opens before you. You see the world with a clarity which for an instant wipes your brain completely blank. Into that space rushes new knowledge: that you are looking down as an experiment, looking down to check that you do not want to jump. A fizzing tremor like a slow-moving electric shock takes your arms, your torso, your legs. And then the scene closes in again, except for the porthole which rises, a gap of light, before your eyes. Through it you see the river bending round towards the City, towards St Pauls' dome. It is still early. You are held, upheld, in a silence that is still the beginning of something. From here the buildings all around you are empty, the glass-sided floors, their lifts and their boardrooms still asleep. But they are beginning to steep themselves in the day's sun. They glisten from the top down, and you follow that spreading light with your eyes until you come to the river gliding smoothly out from under the bridge and it is edged with gold. You grasp onto that golden rim, you pull, you pull again, and then you are through.

The soft rising in your body bursts up through your

throat and out through your mouth and you vomit past your hands and into the water below. And 'I forgive myself' you hear a voice cry.

You reach out and you draw the soft pale blue sky in handfuls towards you, twisting and turning it as you pull and following the morning's golden weft with your eyes. You cup its rich, light glimmer to your body. And then all at once you are content and you are still.

All around you on the bridge commuting pedestrians are glancing in alarm at the girl who was shaking and looking so hard at the water. Now her shoulder is being patted, patted, patted by the tramp in dirty purple. No-one approaches. Slowly the girl draws her neck and head back until she is no longer arched like a slim perched heron. She looks down at the tramp's hand with its gaudy junk-shop ring. The girl shakes her head more firmly as though to prepare for flight. Then, 'come on, my dear, come on,' the tramp says. 'I called and you came and now we will go for tea.'

IV

I take you by the hand and lead you back across the bridge and along the wide Embankment. We shuffle, you and I; not the clean clip of a heel-led stride but always on the balls of our feet, destabilising, brushing the paving and only then our near-silent heels. Your eyes are on the gum-pocked, fast-food-stained concrete slabs. Their surface is roughened with tiny mould-formed blisters; as though the ground, too, is poisoned and dying. Pigeons pick at the night's spatterings of vomit. We walk on. Past the gaudy-swirled shrouded fairground rides, and the immense, near-immobile wheel of the London Eye. Your eyes are steadfastly forward and down; so I admire the view for you. The stalls, I say, are just opening for the day. I point out to you the source of the waffle-smell and that of burned sausage, the protected effervescence of bagged candyfloss and the Union Jack knick-knacks which are so bright, so precarious against the backdrop of heavy sluicing water. We walk through the glister and tinsel. Then abruptly I turn down a side-street and the pretence of entertainment falls away. We are suddenly somewhere dark, dirty, gritted and quiet even in the rush hour: it is under the darker arches of Waterloo station that I take you into the place which I now call home.

We pass through the peeling door and I nod at the girl who sits at the reception desk, her loose-cabled sweater ratted with river-weed dreadlocks, a scarred piercing in her lip and smudged shadow around the whole of her eyes. You look at her and you shudder. She opens her mouth as though in response, but as I say 'sshh' she closes it again. We shuffle, you and I, still unsteady, down the strip-lit corridor. There is a tidemark on the paint at shoulder height; someone has painted the corridor once and only half again. You do not see this. We turn into the dark-floored hall at the end. (It could be any church hall. Anywhere where there is no longer a church.) Still by the hand I lead you, my proud possession, to a rough-grained plastic bucket seat in the furthest corner.

'Sit down,' I tell you, 'and I'll get some tea. Won't be a moment. The water is in tanks. It is always hot.'

I pick out two mugs: red for you and blue for me. I lever the water onto the dusty teabags, pick the cleanest spoon from the pile on the side and stir them round. I add milk from a carton—it gulps out, semi-solid—and then a white sachet of sugar apiece.

Your head has dropped onto your arms so your hair flows cape-like across your whole upper body. It does not really matter. There is no-one here to see. But all the same I pull your shoulders up, watch your head rock back and then be held, teetering, on the bruised stem of your neck.

You stabilise.

I hand you your mug and watch as you cradle it in cold hands. There is a chip in the rim, a grainy beige slur on the red gloss. I want to tell you to mind your lip on its rough edges. But I am silent. I wait.

I wait.

When you are ready you begin to talk.

At first you get all your tenses wrong. Though you remember what has happened since you saw me last as you bade farewell to the ward and you know what you want to say you have nonetheless forgotten the order. You bring no structure, no artistry, no sense of suspense. You maim your own tale. But that is OK. We can push and we can pull over what has happened, and when, and why, and to whom, and what it means. For a while we do. But then gently we find we are tuning into a flow which becomes agreed words, sentences, paragraphs. We know each other well, you and I. We are two melodies intertwined. My words become yours. And yours, torn from your body with such pain? They, my darling, they become mine.

And that is all it takes. We have been drinking tea here now for several days. Always at this corner table, always out of sight. You have wept and shaken and mopped your face with my lace-edged handkerchief and with the greasy serviettes which are stuffed in handfuls between the crusted bottles of ketchup and sauce. I also have cried a little. Now I feel we are ready to face the world.

And so, 'shall we start again?' I, your humble storyteller, ask you. Then, 'No,' I say, and 'not again.'

'We will end there,' I say with a gentle shudder. And you look suddenly startled and you then acquiesce and are at peace.

So let me tell you finally that I have closed my book. I have laid my pearl-ringed hand across it like a seal. I look up and for an instant I smile at you in sorrow. And then your tale is done.

Acknowledgements

Sarah Mortimer, Katie Murphy, Craig Raine and Nick Shuttleworth – who read drafts, commented, and saved me from embarrassment.

Charlie Hall – for reading the text, loving it, and putting me in contact with Robert Peett; and for all of his encouragement and support.

Robert Peett – for having faith in me, giving me confidence, and editing my words so deftly and gently.

Coram Williams and Cynan Jones – for helping me to understand the publishing world.

Gioia Ghezzi, Bridget Luff and many others – for sharing this story with their friends.

Matthew Armstrong – for everything.

ABOUT THE AUTHOR

Kate Armstrong was born in 1979 and grew up in the North of England. She studied English Literature at Oxford University, first at New College and then at Merton, where she wrote her DPhil on John Donne. She also held a lectureship at St Hugh's. Kate then followed a career in international business, writing her first novel, *The Storyteller*, on trains and flights and in hotel rooms. She is currently working more comfortably on her second.

Lightning Source UK Ltd.
Milton Keynes UK
UKOW02f1502220416

272771UK00003B/13/P